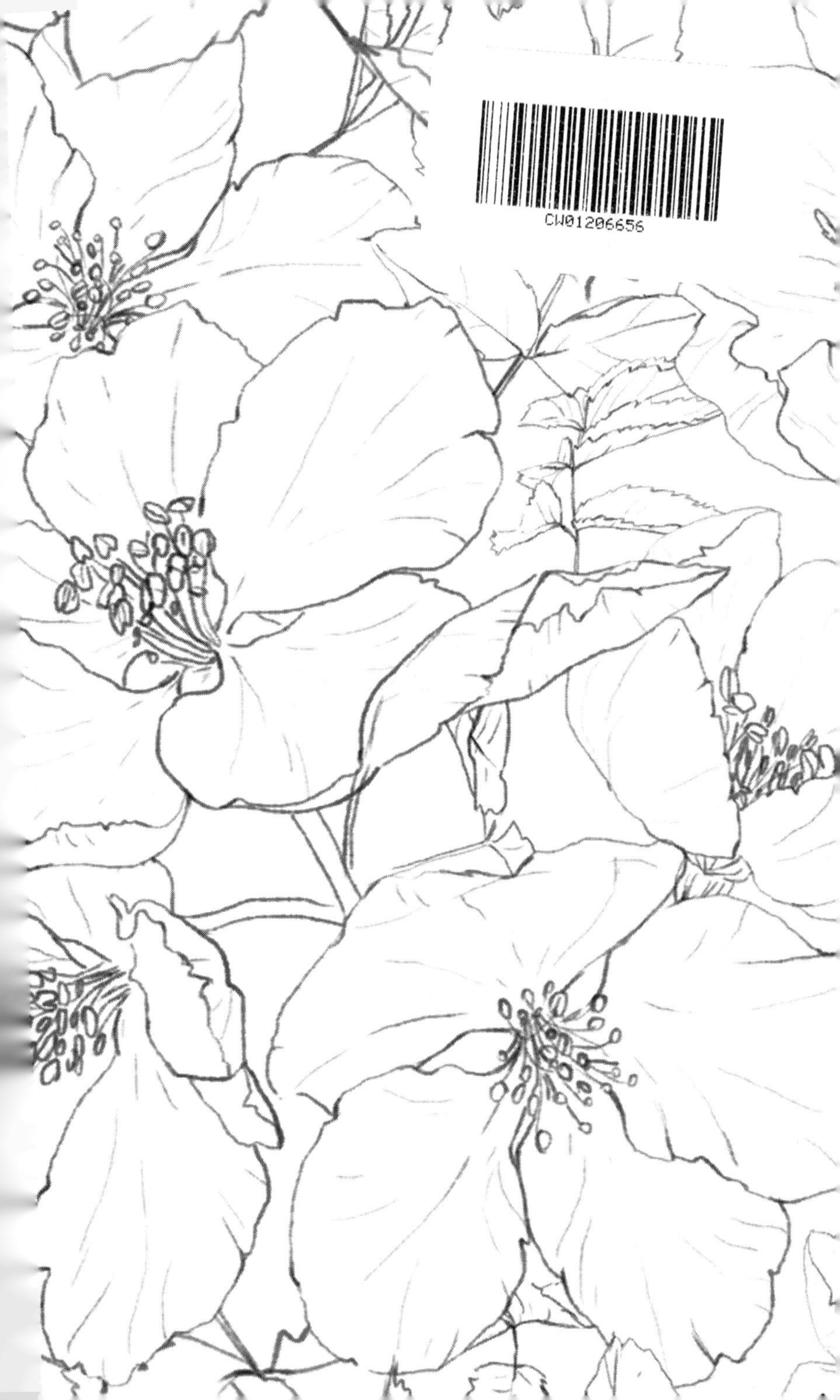

No part of this publication may be reproduced, stored in a retrieval system, or transmitted in any form or by any means, electronic, mechanical, photocopying, recording, scanning, or otherwise, without the prior written permission of the publisher, except in the case of brief quotations within critical reviews and otherwise as permitted by copyright law.

NOTE: This is a work of fiction. Names, characters, places, and incidents are a product of the author's imagination. Any resemblance to real life is purely coincidental. All characters in this story are 18 or older.

Copyright © 2023, Willow Winters Publishing. All rights reserved.

Gabriel & Kiersten

Willow Winters & Lauren Landish
Wall Street Journal & USA Today Bestselling Authors

From USA Today best selling authors Lauren Landish and Willow Winters comes a seductively, addictive, standalone romance.

I had everything.
Wealth, power... and her.
It started as an irresistible and provocative game. Only elite circles knew about the club and what happened behind closed doors.
A monthly auction. A high price bid. A woman I was never supposed to fall in love with.

I taught her what submission is and she loved it more than I could ever imagine. It was perfect... like we were made for each other.

One tragic night tore her from me and there wasn't a damn thing I could do about it.

For years, I've waited. I thought I could have her again. I thought the past wouldn't catch up to us... I couldn't have been more wrong. I brought danger to her doorstep, but I'll burn it all down before I'll ever let her go again.

Bound

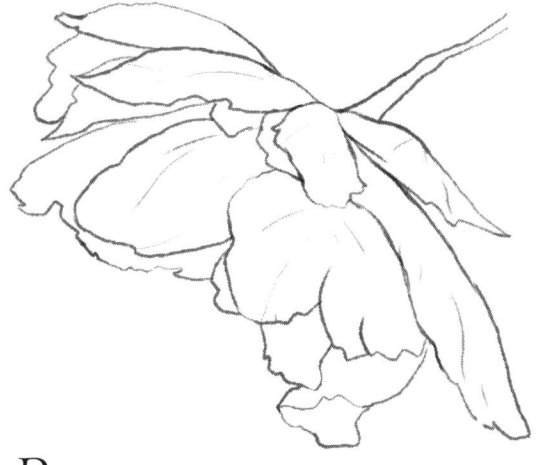

Prologue

Gabriel

Years ago ... when she was mine to do with as I pleased.

That sweet moan of hers is addictive. It spills from her lips easily while he fucks her. With every thrust, his hips force her lush ass to jiggle and her body sways slightly. With her dark hair in curls fallen around her shoulders, her bare back is visible. The velvet dress is an emerald puddle beneath her on the sofa. The thigh-highs held up by clips from her garter belt are a nice touch, though. One I chose myself.

I loosen my tie with one hand, my other hand still on her breast, kneading and plucking her hardened nipple. He's the first of three tonight. The deal I made with Mr. Daniels is worth fourteen billion. His crisp, tailored suit that lies like rags on the floor reeks of wealth, and still, I'm worth more than every man in this room combined.

He almost fists her hair. He reaches, but the bastard catches himself just before. Thank fuck for his jaw's sake that he does. They're not allowed to touch her in any way other than their cock in her cunt and their hands on her hips. No kissing, no extracurriculars, so to speak. That's the rule she proposed and the one that drew me to her. If only she knew who I was and what she was signing up for . . .

"You like that, my little whore?" I murmur, my stiff cock pressing against the zipper of my suit pants.

"Yes Sir," she barely manages as he fucks her harder. His blunt nails dig into her lush hips as he searches for his release, and a possessiveness I've never felt before comes over me as she calls out my name. It's nearly strangled, wrapped up in her pleasure.

My lips find hers, kissing and nipping as my heart races faster. Our touch is short-lived as she braces herself, both hands gripping the arm of the warm brown leather sofa. The scents of whiskey and cigars linger, even if the poker cards are scattered across the floor.

We've done this more than a dozen times. Poker nights with my business acquaintances. She enjoys their touch, and I enjoy watching. She's sensitized by the time I bring her to my room, cuff her to my bed, and punish her.

The other night, she came from my simply blowing on her cunt. That's how high this gets her.

"Gabe!" She cries out my name, reaching up as the men change behind her. She reaches for me, her small fist grabbing my shirt.

My little submissive, being so fucking inappropriate in front of our guests. It takes everything in me not to shove him aside and take her right then and there.

Her half-lidded eyes find mine and then close in utter rapture before she forces them open. That possessiveness rocks through me again, refusing to be ignored. I watch her as she comes on his cock, her lips parted and lust written in her expression. Her hand tightens on mine in a desperate attempt to keep me close.

If only she knew there wasn't a chance in hell I was moving an inch from her. Every muscle is coiled, adrenaline surging through my veins. She's mine. Mine to enjoy, mine to share, mine to cherish.

"Gabriel," she cries, pleasure rocking through her, and I can't take it anymore.

That was years and years ago, but the memory stays with me, nearly hauntingly. I wonder if it's only once in a lifetime that you know the moment you fall in love.

In that moment, I knew I'd have done anything to keep her as mine. I'd have killed for her. I couldn't have imagined the tragedy that would tear us apart. I had no idea I'd kill more than once for her. I never could have prepared for what was about to happen.

Chapter 1

Kiersten

Present Day

The keys jingle in the darkened alley as a chill blows by. It makes logical sense that on the anniversary of the darkest day of my life, I'd feel a prickle creep up the back of my neck. The metal bites into my hand as I grip the keys harder and turn, expecting to see someone watching me. There's no one, though. Not a soul exists beyond myself, and I remind myself that it's only the nerves. It's only the memories that haunt me.

Memories that take me back to another life. Another name, even. Back to when I was only Kiersten, a naive submissive who couldn't have prepared for what fate would do to me. Long before I was ever Madam Lynn.

It's only my past that I'll never outrun. With a steadying breath, I open the heavy side door to Club X.

As I step into the warm hall, with my purse in the crook of my arm and the large hot coffee in my right hand, sin disguised as luxury greets me. An easy smile slips onto my lips. This place is my escape, my livelihood, my sanctuary from everything that waits for me outside these doors.

Warmth greets me as I take in the foyer and lobby on my right and the darkened ballroom on my left.

The click of my heels is muted as I step onto the thick, dark red carpeted floors. Club X is a fantasy come to life and a gateway to another world. One so many people will never know exists, let alone experience. Every detail is meticulous and exudes luxury. The golden sconces give a decadent glow to the place as I flick the light switch on. The light barely reaches the high ceilings, by design, to add to the feel of a fantasy.

As I pass the dining room, I take a moment to ensure the tables were set last night. In only a handful of hours, this room will be filled with rich men, easily poured alcohol, and the finest dining served by white-gloved waiters.

Beyond the velvet-covered booths, the thick red curtains that guard the stage in the back will remain closed today.

The next auction hasn't been announced, but they all know it's coming.

Wealth and anonymity are required for members who bid at the auction.

Curiosity and willingness are a must from the women who are curated and invited to partake in these exclusive events. It's a lust-filled fever dream for many, an irresistible temptation for others, and a potentially life-altering opportunity for all involved.

It's an honor and a privilege and yet... a constant reminder for me. Taking the iron spiral staircase up to the second floor to my office, I remember a time when all of this was only a dream to me. Something I thought would lessen the pain of my wounds, in a way. Stopping short of my office door, I lean my back against the wall and take in a deep, steadying breath.

Today will always be a heavy date, but reminders of him are everywhere in this place, and recently, more often than not, I've felt as if maybe, after so many years, it's time to let go. It's been so long, and although I deal in the world of fantasy, I don't want to live in one myself.

Shaking off the nerves, I open up the door and go about my tasks as if it's any other day. My purse and tweed coat are hung on the metal hooks in the closet, and my golden heels click on the white-washed wooden floors of the office. Apart from the blush wingback chair, the blood-red velvet curtains that line the back wall, and a pale pink damask wallpaper on the right side, everything in my office is a bright white. Even the roses are white in their crystal vase. They're delivered weekly, and the soft scent carries through the long days.

My carved wooden desk is new. It's curved, with two clear, yet comfortable chairs that cost a fortune. They're modern and transparent. Every inch of this place looks and feels expensive. And that's because it is.

My typical deep red attire, in the form of cashmere dresses and silk blouses tailored just for me, fits right at home with the image of femininity yet confidence and power. Today, though, my black V-neck dress stands apart from the softness of my office.

I take a sip of the barely still hot coffee before setting it down on the coaster and bringing my computer to life. Just as I think to myself that the cheap cardboard cup should be replaced with a porcelain cup before anyone arrives, the screen flicks on and there's a knock at the office door.

Curse my desperate heart. For a moment, a fraction of a moment, I think *it's him.* The treacherous thought lingers a second too long before I swallow down the foolishness. Hating my lovesick thoughts, I clear my throat and call out, "Come in," knowing all too well that it's only my security team.

I half expect it to be Joshua, a good friend and partner and the only other person who knows almost everything. He knows enough . . . more than enough. It's a foolish thought, though. There isn't a reason that he'd be in this early.

"Madam Lynn," he greets me with a tilt of his head, both hands shoved into his hoodie jacket. Dressed all in black, he appears somewhat intimidating at the moment. But under the hoodie is a collared shirt, and the moment he smirks, charm takes over all appearances. "It turned winter overnight, huh?" Holden is a twenty-two-year-old kid. With bright blue eyes and a handsome face, he's as charismatic as he is brutal.

"Your knuckles have healed well," I comment agreeably, making a note to lift a brow as I spot the bruised skin. When I met Holden, he was broken down and seemingly damaged beyond repair. He needed a distraction and a second chance.

A client once told me I'm a collector of broken birds. My gaze slips to a small wooden bird painted white that sits next to my computer. That client, a beautiful young woman needing only a chance to escape, gifted me the bird the week she got engaged. *With love, we will all fly again* is engraved on the bottom.

It's not that I pitied Holden. I needed someone on my security team who would blend in. Someone nonthreatening. Someone young to offer a different feel for the women who were intimidated by the other men on my team. All he needed was a hot shower, a good night's rest, and a sharp suit.

It was a partnership that we entered into and one that has played out exactly as I intended.

"Knuckles and" —he turns to show off his freshly shaven and sharp jaw— "no more bruise." He smirks, and I huff a laugh. "Wonderful, although I don't think the ladies minded your stubble."

He chuckles, and as he does so, I ease into my chair.

"So for today," he starts and then runs down the events and who will be on schedule. I nod along, although I already know.

My fingers slip up to my collar bone, and the tips of them travel along the thin chain of my necklace. It's a habit, a soothing one.

Holden has earned his keep and is slowly taking over the management of security. I'm a bit controlling and obsessed with details, but I have to admit, slowing down and allowing others to come in and take over have been a blessing and a curse.

The more time I have, the more time I have to think. Work is my coping mechanism. If I don't have it, I'm only left with memories.

"Madam Lynn?" Holden's voice hitches slightly, gathering my attention.

"Oh, yes, I'm sorry. Could you repeat that for me?" Readjusting, I cross my legs and square my shoulders.

"I just asked if you were alright?"

"I'm fine," I answer and correct my expression.

"You just look a little . . ." His voice drifts, and I finish his sentence.

"Lost in thought?"

"Sad," he corrects.

"Oh." My tone reflects my surprise.

"You want to talk about it?" he offers.

He's used me as his therapist more times than I can count. I don't tell anyone my secrets, though. They're too dark and too heavy a burden for anyone else to carry. I've confided in him before after late nights and a glass of Cabernet . . . or three. But some thoughts I'll never breathe to life. Not even in times like these when I feel so desperately alone.

"I'll be fine, dear," I reassure him with a small smile. "What I want is to get the day moving."

With a reluctant nod, he lets me know that he's there for me if ever I need him. Holden is kind, but he's not the man I need. Certainly not on a day like today.

Chapter 2

Gabriel

Present Day

The first snow of late fall is gentle, yet the cold is brutal. I hardly notice either. I can only watch *her*. The parted curtains barely offer me a view of my submissive, my life, my Kiersten, but it's enough to satisfy my desperate need.

I'm certain she couldn't imagine that anyone would see her lounging in her silk nightgown. The building facing her windows has none of its own, but from the rooftop, I've got a perfect view of her.

She holds a glass of red wine that goes down far too easily. My palm itches to take it from her and part her lips with something else. A low groan vibrates up my chest as I remember those hazel eyes. How she'd peer up at me, craving approval as her cheeks hollowed and she did exactly as she was told.

The memory fades, and in front of me, the woman who loved me with everything she had stares aimlessly at a fire that casts shadows down the side of her face.

I've watched her for days now, longing to hold her, to take away that look of despair she wears when no one is watching.

She's still the beautiful woman I remember. Every detail about her is the same, yet different.

Time has passed, and it's not been forgiving to me, but her beauty is timeless.

She never asked for me to come back, and for all she knows, I died long ago. That night has haunted me since the moment I went into hiding. Since the day I did what had to be done and left to protect her.

I've never wanted anything other than to keep her safe, but at this moment, all I want is to take her on that sofa. To lift the silk fabric up her thighs and command her to spread her legs for me.

I don't have much of a view as it is, and with my hands going numb from the cold, I'll need to leave sooner rather than later. The moment she leaves in the morning, though, I'll be able to search her place for clues as to who Kiersten has become while I've been away.

Patience. I've waited years to come back to her. I can wait just one more day.

The phone in my pocket buzzes, and it takes everything in me to rip my gaze away from her. It's a message from my contact, Roland. He has the background check on her ready and offered to locate her.

My message back is simple. *I already found her.*

The Past, January

Our First Month Together

Seeing my little submissive on her knees is a sight that would unnerve most men. Kiersten's plump lips stretch as she wraps them around my cock, slowly pushing herself down further.

"That's it," I tell her, humming in pleasure as she pushes further. "Take it all the way."

When she'd told me that she'd never deepthroated a cock before, I knew it was one of the first lessons I wanted to teach her.

She's pushed herself, and as her nose gets closer and closer to the base of my cock, I can see her face flush with arousal and an eagerness for more.

Her cheeks hollow, and my toes curl as the tip of my cock presses at the back of her throat and then downward.

"Pull back," I command in a groan, and she does, taking a deep, gasping breath as she pulls off, spit tumbling from her lip as I take her chin in my hand and lift her eyes to look at me. "You're going to take it all, aren't you?"

"Yes Sir," she says breathily. "All of it," she adds with a neediness I fucking love.

"Good," I reply, kissing her deeply before pulling back.

"And what do you think should be your reward?" I push a stray strand of hair back as she bobs on my cock, sucking and letting the tip pop out. Fuck, I feel that tingle up my spine. She's damn good at what she does and a fast learner.

She bites her lip, and I know what she wants. We've already fucked once this morning, and I know she wants more. We've only been together a few short weeks, but I know without a doubt that she loves sex, loves trying new things in bed. And I fucking love testing her limits.

I've never known someone with such an insatiable appetite for sex.

"Tell me, my little whore," I warn her softly, giving her a pet name for the first time. I have to smirk as she blushes and tries to hide her smile. She's so much more relaxed than she was at first. We've fallen into a rhythm and I fucking love it. "Never hide the truth from me. It's one way to immediately get punished."

"I know, Sir," she answers and clears her throat. "I want to look into your eyes as you fuck me in the bed, Sir."

I smile, stroking her cheek. "Is that all?"

"And I want to kiss you, Sir. As we fuck."

It takes everything in me to hold my composure. She's a greedy girl. But romance . . . she knows that's off the table.

"You want me to make love to you?" I ask her, very much uncomfortable. She's asking a dangerous thing. What she wants isn't just sex or fucking.

She shakes her head slightly. "It doesn't have to be that."

Doesn't have to be, but that's what she wants. Hesitation pricks its way through me.

"How about at the very end of the night, I bring you to bed and I fuck you that way? Hmm?" I offer, knowing damn well that I plan to use her up all day today. I have no other plans other than to fuck every hole she has. "Would you like that? If I take you to bed that way?"

"Yes," she whispers, and I lean back on the sofa, spreading my legs and allowing her to get back to the task at hand.

She doesn't hesitate. She swallows my cock again. In seconds, I'm groaning in pleasure as she hollows her cheeks around my shaft. "You love my dick, don't you?"

"Mmm-hmm," she hums, the vibrations adding to my pleasure. She pushes further, swallowing, and with one stroke, she swallows my cock down her throat until her lips have fully wrapped around the base of my cock, my dick buried in her throat. She swallows, massaging my tip with her throat muscles, and I throw my head back.

I can't get enough of this woman. "I could see you enjoying getting fucked right now while you suck me off."

Kiersten pulls back, my dick popping out of her mouth as well. "Sir?"

I read it in her eyes and the way she pants, her chest rising and falling. "You'd like that, wouldn't you? Sucking me while getting fucked?"

"I . . . I've fantasized about that," she admits. "I didn't want to tell you."

I nearly laugh at her thought of not telling me. I'm her Dom. It's my pleasure to see that hers is met.

"You thought I'd be angry, didn't you?" I ask, stopping her before she can go back to my cock by gripping her chin in my hand.

Her gaze struggles to stay on mine before she nods.

"Tell me."

"Yes Sir, I thought you'd be . . . upset or angry at the thought of another man involved."

I chuckle deep and low, my cock twitching with need.

"But I'm not . . . my little whore." I repeat the nickname, and her bottom lip drops slightly, her cheeks flushing with desire at the term, and I know I've hit close to her deepest fantasy.

"I've never told anyone that before, Sir."

"We have time in this month . . . and the next, if you'd like," I remind her, lifting her to her feet. "So tell me all your fantasies. I want to make as many as I can come true."

Chapter 3

Kiersten

The Past, May

A slightly familiar shiver goes through me as I look through the thin black curtain, out at the stage. It's small, just large enough for one person to stand, like a mannequin on display. It's all black, and faint lights line the inside edge of the short runway and circular end, giving anyone who walks onto the stage both sure footing and total illumination.

There are no flaws that can possibly hide between those lights and the overhead spotlight that illuminates the woman at the end of the stage right now, not that she needs to worry. She's a sculpture of a would-be goddess, her flat, toned stomach glittering with a single diamond stud, her long legs lightly tanned, her breasts high and proud on her chest. Even her long, raven's wing hair is a fantasy, framing a triangular face with plump lips and a button nose.

"Don't think about her or them," *he* whispers in my ear, placing a warm hand on my shoulder. My heart races. He's snuck back again. It's not normal for a Dom to be backstage with his submissive. He shouldn't be back here at all. He hasn't bought me yet, either, but I still know I belong to him. "You are the most beautiful woman in the world, my little whore."

"You'll be in the crowd?" I whisper back, and his warm chuckle tells me not to worry. How can I not worry, though? I only want him and he knows it. This auction is for him. Our fifth time. If it were up to me, I wouldn't live a day without his collar on my neck.

He kisses my neck and reassures me that I am his. His promise calms me and gives me enough strength to reach up and move my hair, letting him remove the collar from around my neck.

The first time I went up on this stage, I thought I would never accept a collar. I was desperate, tens of thousands of dollars in debt just as the market collapsed in my chosen field. How was I to know that dot-com was going to go dot-bust?

I'd invested everything. Not just what little money I had, but my education as well. In a single day, I was worth less than nothing. The auction was a way out from debts I couldn't pay back.

That first night I saw him in the crowd, something shifted inside me, even though he was anonymous. All of the men are. It's one of the rules this group has. All the men wear masks.

Curiosity turned to need the instant his eyes met mine.

Even with his mask, I could sense something from him. Those gray-green eyes burned with a power and intensity that drew me like a moth to the flame, more powerful than the clearly expensive tuxedo jacket he wore advertised. He was the sort of man who could control a room with just his eyes while wearing a dirty old T-shirt. It didn't matter.

The tuxedo was nice, though.

"I'm going to go sit down, my little whore," he says, kissing the back of my neck tenderly. "Remember, this is for fun."

We both know it's more than fun. It's perhaps the best foreplay ever invented. I knew it even as I stood upon the stage my first time, and as I waited for the auction to finish for the woman in front of me, I could already feel the warm tingle between my thighs.

He'll be watching.

My nipples tighten, rock-hard nubs beneath the nearly see-through shift that I'm wearing, and as the final bids for the girl ahead of me come in, my heart races. *He* has bought me before, every month . . . but that almost didn't happen the first time. He's not the only one who craved a submissive who didn't know her boundaries. One who wanted to give up complete control.

Our eyes met, and I could feel our connection. He hadn't bid before then—not many of the masked crowd does—but when his eyes met mine, I felt that connection between us. A bidding war took place, staggering me as numbers that I never thought possible were tossed between first four men, then three, then two . . . and finally, just one.

He hadn't won. Not fairly, not with the bidding.

Tonight, though, I know he will. Yes, he likes to share. *Fuck*, it turns me on to be shared, both of us knowing that no matter how passionate, how large or small, how much endurance they have . . . none of them will have the connection that we share.

None of them know my darkest secrets. None of them can command me to do things I never dreamed of and find pleasure beyond imagination. None of them are mine.

He is, though.

Gabriel is my Dom. And tonight is about Gabriel showing everyone, all of these other men, that I am his. It's a heady rush in so many ways, yet my fingertips go numb at the thought of not leaving with him. I assume, like he is, that every man in the crowd is rich and powerful. Knowing that *I'm* the woman they're lusting after, that they want me and will part with even a smidgen of their fortunes in the chance to have me . . . It gives him pleasure to not just own me but to prove to all of the other men that they cannot.

And each of these auctions reinforces that fact while at

the same time enriching me.

"The bidding will open at fifty thousand dollars," the auctioneer, cast in shadow but speaking evenly and with command, says. While these men are bidding on flesh, there is none of the hype, none of the yelling or even descriptions that I thought there'd be.

It is nearly silent, adding to the tension. There are paddles raised and liquor served on silver platters.

If I were to run one of these, I'd do it almost the same way. Almost, but richer and with more attention to detail for the mistresses, the submissives. More . . . security and a promise that the men are getting what they want, but so are the women.

I call myself one of the lucky ones.

One change I'd make specifically . . . a way for the girl to explain herself, her limits, without having to make a speech. These bidders know me now, but the first time, I had to say something.

I'd given speeches in college, presentations in front of entire auditoriums. But telling that room of twenty or so odd men that I'd never had anything but vanilla sex before, but that I was willing to explore, mortified me.

It nearly derailed me, as after the auction, I went to sign the contract that the group required . . . and I found *him* there. There'd been a change of plans as the winner realized that I was not the sort of girl he wanted. So an arrangement was made, a handshake and money exchanged, and I sat across the table from *him* as the auctioneer explained the terms of the contract.

His presence left me breathless, my desire almost as hot as it is now as I stand upon the stage, looking out at the room with a quiet self-confidence. "One seventy-five," the auctioneer says, pointing not toward Gabe but to another. These other men, perhaps they're strong and dominant. Perhaps they are good men too, men who nourish and encourage their women to discover pleasure they never knew.

Perhaps.

But they can't replace him.

Yet he waits, a small, amused smile on his lips as he watches the men lift their paddles time and time again, the price rising past two hundred, past three hundred, past four hundred thousand. My gaze never leaves his, even as my heart races.

When the price passes half a million, only three men remain. I'm sure these are the men I'm shared with, the men who can grip my hips or thighs as they lick at my pussy, the men who grunt and groan and shiver as their dicks thrust in and out of me.

They're good at what they do, and the anticipation of the play time we'll have by the end of tonight has my heart hammering in my chest.

He and I both know that I've nearly climaxed more than

once up here on the stage just from the rush of this moment.

"The price is five hundred and seventy thousand dollars," the auctioneer says, and out of the corner of my eye, I see his head tilt slightly. He has to be wondering, as all the powerful men in the crowd must wonder . . . will this be the time?

Will this be the time that one of them gets to have me?

Is this the time that I become another man's property?

Heat travels along every inch of my skin. "Are there any other bidders?" the auctioneer asks, and in the darkness beyond the spotlight, I can see heads turning, masks looking back and forth. This is what tonight is about. Not the money. By this point, I've paid off my college loans and I have enough to live a comfortable life, with an investment portfolio that's growing by the day.

I could get by the rest of my life without working if I had to.

No, this moment is his gift to me. It's about the thrill, the anticipation.

It's about him teaching me just how powerful I am, and yet all I want is for him to want me, to own me, to refuse everyone else.

"Going once," the auctioneer says, his voice tightening. Yes, we've done this before. Yes, he can guess in his mind what's going to happen in the next few seconds.

But that doesn't stop the tightness from forming.

"Going twice."

Men shift in their seats in anticipation.

"Seven hundred and fifty thousand," he says, his voice brooking no argument. Only once, in all the times that we've done this, did anyone try and up his bid. *He* promptly doubled it, and I have yet to see the mask that risked his wrath in here again.

This time, nobody dares try it, and after three counts and the rap of a gavel, I step away from the stage, my blood still rushing in my ears. In the eyes of the ignorant, they would see me as a whore. After all, I just *sold* myself for three-quarters of a million dollars.

Chapter 4

Kiersten

Present

I keep my desk tidy. Other than the small white bird that serves as a reminder, I don't keep anything that isn't dedicated to business purposes at hand out. Everything has a place, and I know right where it belongs. I've heard people call it austere, spartan, even anonymous. A lot of the people who say that assume it's because of the inherent secretive nature of what occurs here at Club X.

And most of the time, they'd be right. While I've always had a policy of running extensive background checks on all the members of Club X, I'm no fool. I know that when such primal instincts are involved, and then emotions get stacked on top of them, things can get messy. Sometimes even ugly.

But there's one item that is personal, although not many people recognize it as such. Normally, I keep it in my lap drawer, taking it out only on certain occasions. It's a picture of a silver collar, five linked pieces that are so finely crafted that when the collar's closed you can't see the hinges.

In the picture it's locked around a neck, the one carat diamond at the throat dangling against the tanned throat of the wearer, and that's it. You'd have to know me very well to notice the very faint scar above the collar, a scar that came from a tracheotomy when I was only three years old and had an allergic reaction. You can barely see it now.

It healed well, and decades of growth along with a little bit of makeup make it all but invisible. So only a handful of people know that I'm the woman wearing the collar, a picture Gabriel took the day I accepted it and have cherished ever since.

I probably shouldn't keep it here in the office, but I will never remove it. Every time I look at it, I'm reminded of the time in my life when I was content in all things.

Even if it breaks my heart every time I look at it, I will never dishonor myself, my feelings, or what I learned by denying what Gabriel taught me.

On my desk, my phone buzzes, and I stuff down the threatening emotions to pick up the old-fashioned handset. "Yes?"

"Madam Lynn? It's Becca, at the bar. We may have a member who needs attention."

I straighten up, my photograph placed back in the drawer where it belongs, and turn on my monitor. The security office isn't the only place I can see the camera feeds, and with half a dozen clicks of my mouse, four angles of the bar appear, and I can see exactly what the problem is.

Like almost all of the dominant members of Club X, Miles Astor is rich. You don't necessarily need to have a nine-figure bank account to be a member of Club X. There are actually three members, one man and two women, who work nine to five jobs. They're members because they are so skilled at what they do, they thrive here and we thrive with them. The risk in their presence is simple—they don't have as much to lose if events turn unfortunate. They're all too aware, though, that in case we must part ways, I have no limits in what I can do and what I will do if my club is ever threatened.

Every employee is also aware. Assurances are required, and we keep every promise we've ever made.

Miles Astor isn't one of those three members who requires a firmer contract. He's the eldest son and currently the senior executive vice-president at Astor Athletics, a company that gives every high-end sporting clothing company a run for their money in the market.

Like all members of Club X, he was introduced by another, and at the time of his membership, I knew he was a borderline case. Some dominants, on occasion , use their power, their position, their physical stature, and more to bully. He seems to have a preconceived notion that it's simply a part of being dominant. As the old joke goes, shut up or I'll slap you with my wallet.

He's young and naive with much to learn.

But he showed potential, so I approved his membership with the caveat that he learn to, ironically, check his ego and be a proper Dom. He has all the physical tools, six foot two, incredibly handsome behind his mask, with powerful shoulders and a deep, commanding voice developed at Harvard.

But right now, he's in the bar, causing a scene. I rewind one monitor quickly, seeing what happened, and grit my teeth.

He didn't take no for an answer.

There's one golden rule here at Club X. Submissives are submissive, yes. But that submission *must* be earned, even if that often looks and sounds like demands from the Doms. Consent *must* be given. An unattached sub can always tell a Dominant that they are no longer interested. There are always termination clauses in contracts.

And an attached sub? Touching an attached sub is grounds for, at a minimum, suspension of membership, if not expulsion or worse.

Miles didn't go that far, but the rubber membership bracelet on the girl's wrist specifically says that she's an exhibitionist, the blue lefthand ring saying she's unattached by choice. Meanwhile, Mr. Astor wears the bracelet of a full-time Dominant. He desires to *own*, while the submissive in question is here only for à la carte submission. I know exactly why. I know who she is and what her fears are around giving in completely. I've approached Monica with the offer of an auction more than once, but she's declined. I respect her decision.

An expensive membership option, but her choice. A submissive, unless they become a slave, always has a choice. And even then, they have the choice to enter a Master-slave relationship.

I don't have to hear the audio to understand exactly what happened. A man with a bruised ego either retreats or combusts. He made an offer, she refused. It's as simple as that.

The screen shows Mr. Astor slamming his fist on the bar while around the room, other masked men look on in disgust. One approaches him to say something, but Miles turns on him, almost bumping chests with him and shoving him away.

My shoulders bristle with anger as I hold my breath, waiting for security to do their job and minimize the impact.

No doubt, he wants her to enter tonight's auction.

This isn't the first time I've seen pre-auction jitters affect some of the Doms. They want to hand-pick ahead of time and stake claim. It happens from time to time, although it's not always effective. And this isn't the first time I've seen Mr. Astor push the rules of Club X. But he's getting more brazen and poisoning the atmosphere.

That's one thing that I cannot allow.

There's enough conflict inherent in these men's lives. Club X is the place where it is supposed to be set aside, where your status is established in other, subtler ways. Of course, they're going to continue to try and prove themselves. They are individuals who insist that their will must be followed.

My will is what is followed within these walls, though.

I do my best to avoid direct conflict with my members unless necessary. These men are powerful, and if they are willing to commit to a suicidal conflict, they could use their power to destroy Club X.

But it would be mutually assured destruction, as all the members know. I hold immense power throughout not just the city, not just the state, but with members up and down this entire part of the country. I hold power with hundreds of powerful individuals, knowing their darkest secrets and kinks.

Anyone who tries to take down Club X would find themselves crushed by their fellow members. There's always that chance, however, and before things get out of control, I reach for my phone, pressing the pound key twice. "Holden."

"I already have eyes on the bar, Madam Lynn," Holden says immediately without any preamble. *"Would you like me to handle it?"*

"Yes."

"Thank you."

Holden clicks off, and I hang up my phone, my eyes on the monitor.

Holden moves as if by magic through the bar, melting through the tense crowd to appear at Miles Astor's side from the shadows. Even with the high resolution cameras and powerful microphones in the club's security system, I can't make out what Holden says to Mr. Astor, but it's effective. Mr. Astor doesn't look happy, but at the same time, he doesn't cause any more of a scene as Holden escorts him out of the bar and out of the club.

With a gentle nod, the tension leaves my shoulders. *Good.* My to-do list is far too long to have this little moment turn into an unfortunate incident. Tonight's auction requires my full attention, and as I stand up to leave my office, I remind myself who exactly I am to these men. I am not just their equal. I am a woman who holds all the cards, and they must abide by my rules.

As I enter the ballroom, Holden strides in, and with a lift of my chin, I summon him over. We meet at the bottom of the stairs leading up to the auction room. "Yes, Madam Lynn?"

"You handled that well," I tell him quietly, smiling tightly as Holden's chin lifts with pride. "Were there any complications?"

"He wasn't very happy that he was being shown the door, but nothing I couldn't handle," Holden assures me. "Joshua didn't even need to step out from behind his podium."

Joshua is head of security, and occasionally, he positions himself at the front. He was also a co-owner at one point. With more time spent on his family, he's delegated more and more. It's yet another sign of things changing.

I nod, my decision made. "Remove Mr. Astor's access from the systems," I tell Holden quietly. "His membership has been revoked for the time being. I'll message him this evening to inform him of the change and what's required for future entry."

Holden nods, not questioning my decision. His acquiescence is another good trait. Any questions he ever has of my decisions, he saves for the privacy of our meetings in my office. Not once has he ever let a doubt slip from his mouth while in front of other members of Club X.

Holden leaves, and I gather myself a drink at the bar, checking in with the waitress and all those in attendance before tending to what must be done.

Tonight there will be an auction, and for auctions, the preparations must be impeccable. First I find Britta, not far from the bar. She's responsible for the women who will be offered tonight. "How are they?" I ask as I pace the auction room, checking the tables and every detail. They all gleam mellowly in the lighting, which will be softer when it's time to begin.

The stage will be the center of attention.

"Most of the girls are well prepared, Madam," Britta says, handing me an example of the gold-foiled 'menu' that will be offered to our bidders tonight. "But our new girl, Chelsea..." There's hesitance in her tone as she adds, "She's nervous."

I nod, recalling the name. Chelsea is like many of our other submissive women, an invitee who doesn't know quite who she is yet. This is her first auction, her first few days in Club X.

I expected Chelsea's nervousness. However, the fact that she's here so early tells me something, and I give Britta a curt nod. "Have her come see me. It's still a few hours before we open the lounge to our bidders."

Britta disappears, and I tend to the glass of rosé Becca hands me. I must have done this over a hundred times now. And it always weighs heavily. I have to be certain. More certain than the women are who walk across that stage. A moment passes before a gorgeous woman with almost innocent features and a figure that would crudely be described as 'thick' comes out. Her fingers tremble as she approaches me. She fiddles with them by her sides before playing with the hem of her sleeves. "Madam Lynn," she says, dipping her chin in deference. She's new, but she has all the instincts of a submissive inside her already. "Miss Britta said you wanted to talk to me?"

"Yes, I wanted to see how you're feeling," I tell her, looking her over with a professional smile. Either she's got an exquisite eye or perhaps Britta assisted her in picking out the dress that she's wearing, a subtly shaped storm-gray piece made of almost diaphanous lace that reveals her generous breasts. The gray against her beautiful brown skin is perfectly complementary.

She's slightly soft in the tummy area, and her curves add to her gorgeousness. I know that to the discerning Dom, she's going to be his every wish fulfilled. With her long black hair pulled back into a simple ponytail, she's elegant and refined.

"I'm . . . not sure," Chelsea says honestly, reaching up to tuck a stray lock of long, black hair behind her ear. "I'm just . . . nervous."

"That's to be expected." I take a moment to watch her reaction as I sip the wine and then ask, "Nervous about the bids or nervous about what comes after?"

"Both," she answers breathily, blushing slightly.

"Do you understand how things are going to run?" I offer.

She nods again, but it's a rhetorical question. I do this every time with new women, and even seasoned submissives, because I want to always be sure that they've been told the rules.

"I'm just . . ." She swallows thickly, her gaze everywhere but on me as she struggles to tell me what's on her mind. I can already guess it, though, the insecurity of being bid on. The fear of what comes after. I can practically hear her heart running away.

With a kind tone, I reassure her. "Chelsea, they will want you, trust me on that."

"You . . . you think so?" she asks shyly, fingering her rubber membership bracelet. "My friend said so, but I thought she was just being nice. I mean, I'm—"

"None of that, honey," I chide her softly. "And yes, I'm sure. Now tonight, you will be on stage alone, displayed one by one for our bidders. The auction will start at five hundred thousand dollars, and bids go up by a hundred grand a bid." Chelsea squirms, and I lay a hand on her shoulder. "Chelsea, look at me."

She does, biting her lip. "Madam Lynn, I'm—"

"Going to start a bidding war tonight and change your life in the process," I assure her. "And the terms are set by you." My gaze falls to the band she wears on her wrist. Red for pain.

"A red rose still?" I question, although I'm all too sure of her preferences. It's why she was selected. There's a demand for submissives like her, and with this contract, she'll experience pleasure like she's never imagined.

Chelsea nods, her gaze firmly matched with mine this time. "I want pain."

"You'll be holding a red rose to tell the bidders that is your preferred style of play."

She nods again. "I've asked previous boyfriends to go harder, to . . . to spank me. It feels good, but I want more . . . like what happens in the dungeon."

"I know, love," I assure her, smiling again. "Have you seen the pamphlet? Your specific requests and no-go areas we've gone over are laid out in the pamphlet that the buyers will get when they come in. They're also in the contract, and we'll go over it line by line. When it's time to sign, that's the time to make any changes or clarify any points. Your hard limits will be written into the contract."

"I know," she tells me quietly. "I've seen it and thought about it nonstop."

"And you know there will be an NDA, and it is iron-clad, and any violation will be dealt with?"

Chelsea nods. "I know."

"Now the most important part of the contract, Chelsea, is the length. It will be for exactly thirty days, you understand. If you obey all the rules, if you complete your contract, you know what you get, right?"

"Half the money bid on me," Chelsea says, and I nod.

"It's kept in an escrow account. Your buyer cannot take it back unless you violate the contract."

"And if he . . . I don't know, fires me?" Chelsea asks, putting it in terms of employment. I get it. A lot of first-time girls do. "What happens?"

"Then the club investigates. If you didn't violate the contract, you will receive every last cent."

"And if he violates any term of the contract, the same goes. And if you'd rather end it early, you can do so. The money, however, won't be delivered."

"And the men . . . they like this?" Chelsea asks, and I chuckle, leaning in to whisper in her ear.

"Honey, even if you're a bit scared . . . the thought of what lies just beyond a signed piece of paper turns you on, doesn't it?" I ask, and she nods. "How do you think they feel? You're going to have every eye in the room on you tonight. These men will lust for you, yearn for you, and all you have to do is be strong enough, brave enough, to allow yourself to learn what you like, what you want. They will give it to you willingly."

I step back, and she's practically breathless, her large eyes dark with desire. "If anything is concerning, I am a phone call away. Always," I reassure her.

Chelsea nods, biting her lip again, but this time, not in fear but in eagerness.

"Thank you, Madam Lynn."

I pat her on the shoulder, grateful to offer her this. I'm almost certain I know who will leave with her tonight, and I can only imagine how pleased she will be. Hearts break from time to time, but I don't want these women to ever regret doing this. I leave her with the parting, "Enjoy the night."

I do a quick check with the other girls in the backstage area, from the other girl who's also a first-time auctionee but who's been an active 'playtime' member of Club X for nearly a year, to the girl who's amassed a staggering fortune from offering herself for auction three to six times a year. We even have a repeat auctionee, a girl who was like me long ago, re-auctioning herself every month, only to be repeatedly 'bought' by her Dom . . . who I suspect has a ring to match her collar in the not too distant future.

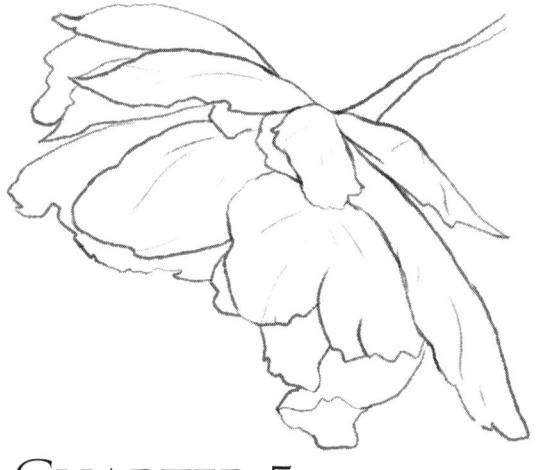

Chapter 5

Gabriel

Present

Everything in her home is soft and feminine, and there's a warmth and luxury in every detail. When I vanished that unfortunate night, I left her enough to never work a day in her life. I left her with security, with enough cash to never want, let alone worry.

And yet, her home is humble in comparison to her means. I went through the background check, her accounting and every detail available. My Kiersten was always sharp. She knew what she wanted and what it would take to get it. She didn't have to compromise on a one-bedroom apartment in a high-rise.

As I open the drawer to a vintage armoire, it occurs to me that she's certainly spent a pretty penny on her home, but even more so on the club.

The knowledge that she's never left the scene makes my throat tighten. My grip is at odds with the dainty glass knob as a possessiveness that I've long controlled threatens to take over.

One truth keeps me steady. Kiersten could have fucked a hundred men in the years we've been apart and I would still be her first. I would still be the man who held her hand as she explored every boundary she dared whisper in confidence. She would still be mine. Her first in every way.

As if an answer to the insecurity and uncertainty that riddles the back of my mind, a picture stares back at me as I open up the second drawer.

A black and white of us. I remember the day I held her back to my front, my hand laid over hers on the railing on the rooftop in New York City. I gifted her a night of five-star dining and luxury she'd never imagined. And in return, that night, she told me she loved me.

My fingertips barely graze the photo.

As the door shuts, the nostalgia vanishes as well.

How do I go back to her? That thought has kept me up countless nights.

She was perfect for me and I for her. If only that night years ago had ended differently.

17 YEARS AGO, MAY

I never imagined life could be this fucking good. The cap of the whiskey bottle twists off too easily, and the auburn liquid pours into the crystal tumbler with a familiar sound.

My little whore's whimpers still linger in the penthouse. As I swirl the glass, staring down at the liquor, I remember what the men agreed on tonight. The million-dollar deals made over cards and reckless bets.

In the business of trading companies and stocks, of buying retail and selling, once the cashflow hits the table, nothing is off limits. Nothing but her.

She's mine. Gorgeous and tempting. A smirk pulls at my lips as I remember the shock on her face as she walked in, red-soled stilettos and black lace lingerie under her winter coat. My sweet Kiersten just wanted to surprise me.

The rough laughter of men comes from the right, where cigar smoke plumes and the game continues. The soft murmurs of Kiersten to my left, where she's still waiting for me to untie her from the lounge chair. It's quite like the horse at the BDSM club, but it blends in far more nicely with the bedroom furniture. If someone wasn't a part of the scene, they'd have no idea until they saw the silk ties.

"You enjoy yourself?" a man says to my left, and I'm brought back to the present.

A rough chuckle leaves me. "If there wasn't a deal on the

line, I'd kick you fuckers out so I could enjoy myself again."

He laughs. Jacob Linds, a man who's a decade older, comes from wealth and enjoys the club just as much as I do. He understands my vice.

"Sir?" Kiersten calls out, and my cock hardens from the lust-filled tone. I can't help the groan as I lower the glass of whiskey and my attention is brought to her.

My gaze moves from the hall back to Jacob. His expression can't hide exactly what he's thinking. He's too slow to change it, and when his eyes come back to me, he lowers them, no doubt ashamed of what he was just thinking.

That he'd like to fuck her too.

I can't blame the man . . . in fact, I fucking love that they want her.

If only he knew what she'd confided in me just the other night.

I take a swig as he clears his throat and pats the counter, ready to leave me and revisit the game room. "You want to see her?" I offer as a soft moan slips from the room down the hall.

Jacob stops on his heel, a questioning gaze finding mine. He glances down the hall and then back to me.

"I told her I'd be back and that she should be ready for . . ." I gesture with the drink in my hand. "Whatever I think she'd enjoy."

Jacob is slow to face me fully, but when he does, he asks, "Is that right?"

"She's a greedy girl," I tell him. "She needs . . ." I take in a steadying breath, knowing what I'm offering and how it could be exactly what she wants or it could backfire. She has her safe word, though, and with that, I'm willing to test her boundaries. "She needs a lot of attention. More than I can offer, I think."

Jacob clears his throat once more. "Well . . . maybe I could offer some assistance? If I could see what it is that she needs attending to." He doesn't outright say it, so I do. "I think you should try her mouth before her cunt."

It only takes a half-second before a slow smirk pulls his lips up. He's none too subtle as he readjusts himself, and I gesture for him to follow me.

It doesn't take long for the other men to filter in, for them to come to a conclusion, although they each ask permission.

"Be a good girl for us, Kiersten," I command her, and those beautiful eyes reach mine.

With Jacob's cock in one hand and the head of it in her mouth, she moans and arches her back, her cunt on full display. "She's needy," I comment to the room as I pace behind her. I grab the flesh of her ass and squeeze. Her moan forces her to lower her head as pleasure and pain ride through her. "Did I say stop?" I question her, and my beautiful little whore is quick to respond.

"No Sir." She bobs her head on Jacob's cock, and his head falls back. It's then that his suit pants fall to the floor and the men behind him let out a chuckle.

Nervously, Kiersten peers up. It's her first time being shared. I'm more than certain that she'll have her insecurities.

"Your mouth is so good, you could bring him to his knees," I murmur in her ear, although it's loud enough for them to hear. At that, Jacob leans forward, his cock falling out of her mouth, and his hand catches his release. He's winded and no doubt enjoyed himself.

"I'm calling it out. You're cheating, Thompson," Daniels says with a touch of humor. "You'll rob us blind if she's on the table," he says and then laughs.

A prick travels up my spine at the comment. As if they could have her. As if she's not mine.

"There's business and then there's business. She's not for sale . . . she's not a bargaining chip. This is simply pleasure. Isn't that right, my little whore?"

With swollen lips and a blush that rises all the way to her temple, Kiersten's gaze seems to pierce into me. A desire and a fulfillment that's sinful takes over her. "Yes Sir," she answers, and I take her chin in my hand, the rough pad of my thumb traveling along her lower lip.

Jacob's back is to us as the zipper is heard, but the other three men are still here, watching and waiting.

I raise my voice as I gently pet Kiersten's back. "Who's next?"

Chapter 6

Lynn

Present

As I shut my car door and hit the alarm, I can't help but feel pride knowing that tonight was remarkably successful. My heels click on the asphalt as I make my way to my building.

Chelsea had, as I'd predicted, lit the auction room on fire, with twenty of the men in attendance bidding for the contract on her. While most dropped out quickly, she fetched one point one million dollars.

She signed a contract with a well-known Dom in the Club, a man who will teach her exactly what she can and cannot take and do it in a way that will help her blossom even more. She has no idea where her boundaries lay, and the man who won her is practically an expert at finding them, and also respecting and enjoying them with his partner.

The warmth I feel from that knowledge is quickly chilled as I step back. With a hitch in my breath, I feel it again, that prick up the back of my neck. It's eerie, and even when I turn my head from side to side, checking the street and seeing nothing, it's still there.

This is worse than every on and off feeling I've felt throughout the week. My first inclination is that it could be Mr. Astor. I anticipated a reply the moment I emailed but got nothing. I peer out into the night and through the concrete garage. My heart races and my pace picks up. I walk as quickly as I can around the corner to the elevator.

I have to remind myself that no one in the club even knows where I live. Joshua does, but only because I knew him before all of this. He's the only one who knows more than the façade that is Madam Lynn. If most members of Club X saw my home, I bet they would be surprised. Most of the members own a penthouse suite or inherited a mansion. They measure their homes by floors, not square feet.

Me? While the Cunningham Towers is a nice building, a modern high-rise that's the tallest in the neighborhood, I don't live anywhere near the penthouse suite. In fact, my apartment is only about two-thirds of the way up the tower, roughly equal with the buildings across the street, a one-bedroom place that I bought when the building was brand-new and I needed to invest every dime I had into getting Club X up and running. I'm safe here too, with security watching.

Even knowing that I'm safe, that there's no one watching me, that no one could have followed me home when the streets this late at night are barren . . . I can't put my finger on it. I trust my instincts. Reaching for my phone, I quickly text Holden. *I want security increased at the Club. Fifty percent increase until further notice.*

I hit *Send*, not expecting a reply, but I'm slightly reassured when I get an almost immediate reply. *Done. Everything okay?*

My breath turns to fog in front of my face as I near the building. With my keys between my knuckles, the ones that dangle jingle.

I only hesitate a second to text him, *I feel off.*

Do you need help now?

I look around the parking garage once more and think logically, pushing down the fear and the wreck of emotions that's plagued me this week. My building has security. The only way to get into the parking garage is with a key card or a remote control. And from here, I can take the elevator straight to my floor, where my door is right across from the elevator.

No, I text back. *Just cover the club. If I need help, I'll call.*

Understood, Madam.

With my throat tight and the tip of my nose cold, I tighten my grip on my purse, keeping the remote in my hand, my thumb poised over the panic button that'll not just send my horn into a fit, but also call both the cops and Club X security.

Better safe than sorry.

But nobody accosts me before the elevator closes, and the hum of the motor drawing me upward helps relieve my tension. True, someone could try and jump on with me at one of the other floors, but at this time of morning, almost everyone's going down, not up.

Relief is slow to greet me, though. I can't shake the feeling, and I remind myself that work is how I cope. The auction was a distraction and now it's over. As the elevator pings with each floor, my stomach drops. There isn't enough money in the world that can help what my mind does this late at night.

I force my shoulders to relax. I know I have a bottle of wine or sleeping pills that will turn these thoughts off.

Everything is okay. I'm okay . . . I remind myself, although nothing feels okay.

I should be relaxing, but instead, as the elevator rises higher and higher, the feeling intensifies. As I approach my floor, I know that I'm going to rush inside my apartment, triple-lock my door, and if I can't get to sleep immediately, drain an entire bottle of that Greek red wine I've got that puts me to sleep quickly.

I unlock my door and enter as quickly as I can, immediately turning around to do all my locks. First the thumb bolt, then the twist lock, and finally, I stand on my tiptoes to push the vertical posts into place. Just as I feel the inch-thick steel post slide home in its sleeve, I feel something . . . someone behind me, and I spin. "Who—"

Shock and terror grip me as I turn, but then I'm paralyzed. My words dry on my lips as I see . . . *him.*

With a chill running down every inch of me, I can't believe what I'm seeing. This is just another hallucination after a long day on a sad anniversary, but when I open them again he's still there, black pants, white dress shirt, his black tie slightly undone just like he used to when we were alone. Older, with faint wrinkles around his eyes, but the way he looks at me . . . My Gabriel.

"Is . . . is it you?" I whisper, my knees trembling. Tears threaten to spill down my cheeks, my chest aches with a breath I can't seem to take, and as he steps forward through the soft security lights that I leave on when I'm gone, he says nothing, and it isn't until he's right in front of me and I've backed up against my front door that I know I'm not imagining things.

"Please," I whisper, my tears falling. "Is it you . . . Sir?"

His lips twitch, and he reaches out, tucking a lock of my hair behind my left ear just like he used to. His touch is like fire. "Hello," he says, my knees unlocking as the voice I thought I'd never hear again outside of my dreams is whispered at the shell of my ear. "It's me."

Chapter 7

Gabriel

Present

"It's me."

I don't know what else to say. I haven't felt this fucking nervous since I last looked over my shoulder and boarded a flight to get the hell out of town. Not since I said goodbye to her. I swallow thickly and take a single step forward, ignoring the battering in my chest.

Maybe on the outside I'm cool, calm, and collected, with no real issues about standing in her apartment, waiting for her as if I belong here. But the truth is that I'm burning up on the inside.

A slow prickle creeps up the tips of my fingers, and I itch

to touch her, to have my hands on her body and bring her in close. I'm perfectly still, though, as she stands there in complete shock.

I thought I was ready. I thought that after seeing her from afar, and seeing her through the lens of the investigators I paid to tail her, that I'd be ready for her. The truth is . . . nothing could have prepared me for my Kiersten.

Her hair's still silky, maybe with a touch of color in it now to hide a thread of gray here or there, but two decades have treated her as if she's a decadent wine. Her face is still the same, those same large, expression-filled eyes, the same flawless cheekbones, the same soft, plump lips that were made for kissing.

She's still my every fantasy, not just because she's a vision but because of every little piece of her that's been etched into my soul. As I inhale, I can smell that special mix of aromatic spice perfume and natural essence that are entirely her.

"You're still wearing Schernazde," I murmur, referring to the perfume that I introduced her to. "Why?" The question is barely spoken beneath my breath.

She hesitates, and I can see the answer in her eyes. She's done so many things, but she's still *mine.*

Rather than wait for an answer, I let it go. "I let myself in," I continue after a moment, allowing the tension to relax slowly.

She blinks but seems to find her voice again, albeit quietly.

"I can see that."

With one step forward, she has nowhere else to go. Her back is against the door. I can't help it any longer. I cup her cheek, rubbing a roughened thumb across her cheekbone and marveling in how soft her skin still is. Her eyes close slowly, and the softest of sighs leaves her.

That's my good girl.

Her hands cup mine, gripping onto me and keeping us skin to skin. The feel of her is like fire. Soft and gentle, though. It's far different from me, not after all these years. My touch is rough in a way that neither of us were familiar with back then, my fingers callused and roughened by a lifestyle that I saved her from.

They say that the true measure of any choice is knowing whether you'd do it again even with full hindsight to your benefit. And well, here I am, and I'd make the same choices again if I had to. "Kiersten."

She swallows thickly, her eyes focusing after another breath, and the questions pour from her as if they've been held in for a decade. "Where did you go? How did you get here? How did you know where to find me? Why did you come here? What happened, is everything—" Her tone becomes hectic, and the worried look I left her with returns.

I cut her off before she can devolve into full panic mode, pressing my thumb to her lips. "Shh." Her gaze is locked with mine, wide and panicked, so I do what I must . . . I lie.

"Everything is fine."

"Fine?" she questions, her eyes still slightly glassy even though her eyebrow rises incredulously. "Gabriel, you disappeared from my life. I heard nothing, knew nothing for close to twenty years . . . and everything is fine?"

I nod, knowing I'm hiding the full truth from her. I never want to burden her with all of the darkness, all of the sin, that I've carried since I left. "You know I had to," I remind her, hoping that will be enough.

She knows the basics. She knows *why* I had to disappear. Why I had barely enough time to do much more than turn a few financial accounts over to her, enough to set her up for life . . . or to open Club X. I still have questions there, details that I want answered.

"Everything is fine," I repeat and add in a calming tone that used to soothe every worry she had, "I wouldn't be here if it wasn't."

A moment passes, and I watch as her guard slowly lowers, as her expression softens, but not so much that she's amenable.

"So what does that mean?" she asks, uncertain, unsure . . . untrusting. It's that last bit that hurts. I swallow thickly. She used to trust every word that came out of my mouth. If I'd told her to jump from the top of a skyscraper, she'd have done it with full trust that I'd have a way to swoop out of the sky and catch her before she got hurt.

Not an ounce of anger surfaces, only desire to have it back. All I've ever wanted was her. Every bit of her. It's been a very long time, and I have to re-earn what's been eroded by time. "It means I could be back," I tell her quietly. "We could be together again."

"Could be?" she asks, and I only nod.

"If you want," I add. "I won't say I'm happy to see the worry in your eyes, Kiersten. But I'm not stupid. I know that we won't be like we were before. We're different people now. But different doesn't mean I don't still want you with every ounce of my soul."

I step back, releasing her from my touch and letting her decide. It takes everything in me to turn, giving her by back and walking to her living room. I prepare myself for whatever may come before turning around to look at her again. The soft morning light is just starting to filter through her curtains, and I can see as her expression softens even more.

She steps further into the apartment, dropping her purse onto the table, but she doesn't stop watching me. Only then does she quiver, taking a deep breath before turning away to stare at the wall to compose herself. "It's been almost two decades, Gabriel."

"I know." My voice holds a deep rumble. "It's been so long."

She looks up at the ceiling, taking a deep breath. "I'm still not sure whether you're actually standing there or I'm losing my mind."

"I'm here," I repeat. Disbelief is better than not wanting me, at least. I'll take it.

"I . . . I dreamed of seeing you again," she admits quietly, "but I've never allowed myself to actually believe it was possible. It hurt too much to have hope." She takes another step forward.

"I know what you mean," I admit, and when I do, she takes another step closer. "I spent our first decade apart not letting myself believe this day could happen. Then I've spent the second doing everything I could to simply see you and not risk hurting you." She makes her way over, standing just in front of me, emotion riddled in her gaze as she takes me in.

Adrenaline courses through me as I step forward, wrapping my arms around her waist like I used to and burying my nose in her hair. She relaxes in my embrace, and that's all I need to hold her tightly. Her hair is pulled up, not long and loose like she used to when she was mine and everyone knew it, but it still feels the same, and when I lower my lips to the curve of her neck, she tilts her head, mewling just like she always did when I find the spot on her neck and leave an open-mouthed kiss.

"Sir . . ."

A groan escapes me, rough and from deep in my chest. I'm instantly hard for her.

"Yes, my good girl," I reply, kissing her neck, pacing to the back of her so my chest is pressed against her back. Reaching around her elegant dress, I cup her breast, feeling the soft weight once again mold to my touch. They're softer, maybe a touch larger than they were then, but the nipple that pebbles under my fingertips is exactly the same.

Her soft sigh and the way her hips press back against my hips unlock the years, and for a long moment I hold her, burying my nose in the curve of her neck.

She leans against me, and I squeeze her breast, not hard because my little whore's tolerance has never been high, but just enough that she moans, rolling her hips against mine and stiffening my cock to full attention. She fits into me just right, just like she did back then.

"Bend over the table," I murmur into her ear and then nip her lobe, directing her over to the small dining table near the kitchenette. "Push your ass back . . . the way I like you."

She doesn't answer. She doesn't need to. Her moves are instant. She obeys with a desperate need, bending over the table and lifting her ass in her high heels. My skin is on fire as I push the skirt of her dress up, revealing the provocative but demure silk panties underneath, along with the thigh-high stockings that always drove me wild.

No garters.

Her ass is lush, and as I run my hands along her curves, she sighs happily, pushing into my touch without moving her hands even a millimeter. It's been nearly two decades, and she's still so exquisitely trained.

I bend down, inhaling the sweet scent of her already wet pussy and her earthy aroma as I roll the panties down her long, shapely legs to her ankles, lifting one knee after the next to remove them before setting her leg down a little wider apart, giving me more access.

With a hand on her shoulders, I press her front down so her chest is pressed against the wood and her panting fills the room.

Smiling, I torture my little submissive the way that we both know she likes best, not with hard spanks or bindings but with feather-soft kisses up the backs of her legs to the round peach of her ass, kisses with enough pressure and grazing of my teeth to let her skin know I'm there and sensitize her, but so feathery soft that all she gets is a ghost of stimulation. Goosebumps travel along my touch.

I've spent hours doing this before, covering her entire body from head to toe in these kisses, and more than once, I've made her come so easily on my face with a single soft kiss on her clit at the end. That's how I love her. At the highest of highs and barely cognizant of anything but the touch I give her.

But after all these years of separation, I don't have that patience nor that strength. Instead, I reach out my tongue, stroking her smooth lips and hearing her gasp while my greedy hands undo my pants, freeing my cock. The sound of my zipper being undone fills the small place.

As I stand up and entwine my hand in her hair, I'm lined up perfectly.

"How long?" I rasp as I tease her folds, feeling her ooze over me. "How long since you've been fucked the right way, my whore?"

I shouldn't ask. I shouldn't want to know. She could have fucked her way through all of the state and I'd have no right to criticize, nor would I care to.

But I still need to know. *Did anyone love her right while I was gone?*

"Too long," Kiersten whimpers, and as I thrust forward, I let myself imagine that she's saying something more than she is.

The tight grip of her walls around my cock has my pulse roaring in my ears as I groan out, "Holy fuck." Making sure my grasp is tight, I tug on her hair at the base of her neck to pull her in tighter.

Time loses all meaning as I thrust inside her, feeling her pussy adjust to me, tightening and clenching around me. She pushes to meet my every stroke, both of us knowing exactly what the other needs.

Every thrust is harder and filled with more and more need as I take her ruthlessly.

I don't need to interpret her cries of pleasure. I angle my hips to stroke directly over the places she likes, going harder as her body demands it. She does the same, and as my explosion rises inside me, we find our release together.

She calls my name in utter pleasure, her body shuddering and her pussy clamping around me as we fall apart together.

Chapter 8

Kiersten

Present

Lying in bed, I still can't quite believe it.

He's back.

Gabriel.

My Gabriel.

For years, I've dreamed of him coming back. I've woken up in this very bed hoping he'd be here lying with me. I roll over carefully, and only just so, the bed groans gently in protest. And there he is.

But this is no fantasy.

I can feel him, his arms still possessively around my waist, holding me close, as if he's saying he's never going to let me go again. I can hear his breathing, so missed, against the back of my neck, and when I squirm slightly, I feel his arms tighten. The tips of my fingers play along his corded muscles, slipping through the hair that's scattered along his forearm.

Years feel as if they were only days, and I don't know how time passed without him here.

A simper plays at my lips, and feelings I haven't felt in over a decade threaten to overwhelm me. This man has always had power over me. It's impossible to deny as I lie quietly in his arms, wanting nothing more than this.

"Kiersten," he murmurs. The rough timbre is every bit of what I remember it to be.

It's not a question, but at the same time, it is. I adjust and relax. "I never planned to have anyone in this bed with me. My shoulder's not used to this spot."

He chuckles, and his arms loosen slightly, letting me find a better spot. I turn over, nestling against him, and he kisses the top of my head . . .

Just like he used to.

The ache in my chest tightens as the questions whisper at the back of my mind. So many questions, and I silence them all.

I catch the bottom of my lip between my teeth as he tells me to sleep. It's nearly three a.m., and I know we can talk tomorrow, like he said we would. *How can I sleep, though, when it already feels like I'm dreaming?* Somehow, even though it's been a lifetime apart, I feel like I'm right back where I was . . . all those years ago . . .

Back to that first time, when I almost didn't believe any of this was real.

The Past, February

The iron doors to the private elevator open, and I walk in idly without conscious thought, stunned by the luxury.

A two-floor penthouse with vaulted ceilings in the living room, a 'lounge' that's inlaid in black marble and filled with books, a master bathroom bigger than any home I've ever stepped foot in, complete with a black marble built-in jacuzzi bathtub and gilded faucets, and more.

I can't help the overriding thought that I don't belong here. Even as he tells me where to sit, how to sit, and that I've done so well learning his preferences. I bite the tip of my tongue as I think, *and you've done a damn good job learning mine.*

"It's been thirty days, my little whore," he says as he strokes my cheek, making my nipples tighten and my heart hammer in my chest. Who would have thought, just a month ago, that a single touch would create such a reaction in me? It's him. It's what he's done to me. He plays my body like I was made for him. He knows every button to push because he installed them.

The thoughts that have been torturing me scream in my head. *No one will ever give me what he has ever again. He's ruined me.*

"Yes Sir," I reply, leaning into his touch.

I know I shouldn't ask such questions. It's not my role to ask. It is my role to do exactly what he wants me to do and to accept that. It's my role to follow the rules he's set forth.

And I fucking love it. I haven't a single issue with that arrangement.

But I can't help it, on today of all days. Looking up at him, I need to know. He's been so distant over these past few hours, like he's giving me space for some reason. Only now, as we prepare to go out for the evening, has he called me to him to talk.

On the last day of our contract. Tomorrow, I'm no longer his. Which also means he's no longer mine.

"Have I . . . pleased you?" Nervousness wracks its way through me.

Gabriel blinks and tilts his head. "Why would you think you haven't? You've learned so much about yourself, haven't you?"

I nod, biting my lip as a heat spreads through me. "I have."

"And do you enjoy what you've learned?"

The question stops me, making me think. He's taught me the exaltation of pushing my limits and the peace that comes with accepting that if I let go and allow him to do whatever he wants to me, I can feel pleasure beyond imagination. I've learned that yes, there are times I crave the crack of the crop on my ass, and that a silk scarf wrapped around my wrists is a fucking aphrodisiac.

I've learned just how far I can take his cock all the way into my throat before the world starts to fade, and I've learned how long I can hold my orgasm back before a plug in my ass and a vibrator on my clit make me come so hard I nearly pass out.

I've learned how good it feels to simply say 'yes, Sir' . . . and how much those two simple words convey.

A million lessons, and I owe them all to him. "I love what I've learned," I admit and then realize I said 'love'. Such a forbidden word for a relationship like ours.

And what a stupid thing to say when in twenty-four hours, our time is up and I might never see him again.

"I appreciate your spoiling me, too." I add the comment to distract from my previous reckless statement.

Gabriel chuckles, stroking my shoulder. "I'm glad you liked the dress."

"I've liked everything you've given me," I tell him honestly. "Not just the gifts but the outings and dinners, the experiences, the . . . everything."

Gabriel nods. "You've been amazing as well." His tone is lower and sincere, almost thoughtful.

I swallow, looking down at my fingers that tangle with

one another in nervousness. There's been one thing on my mind, because I know that the contract is over in just a few hours. "Sir, I want to know . . . since the contract is over tomorrow and the auction—"

Gabriel nods, his eyes darkening. "You want to do it again."

I nod worriedly, scared that he doesn't feel the same. After all, he has wealth I never will, experience that's far greater than mine, and the power. He has all the power. "I don't want this to end. I . . . I belong to you. More than the contract." My heart races as I swallow down the question . . . *could I simply be yours? With no end date?*

Gabriel lets out a breath, and after a moment, he smiles. "So that's what's been on your mind all day."

"Yes, Sir."

Instead of answering, Gabriel pushes me back onto the couch we're sitting on, his eyes flaring as his left hand wraps around my throat, just above the lace collar I'm wearing. It's not a full collar, just a regular choker tied at the back of my neck with a simple bow knot, but it means so much to us both.

His lips find mine, crushing me in a powerful kiss and making me want to embrace him, but he's taught me well. I'm instantly breathless. I hold onto the cushions of the couch as he presses into me, his right hand reaching between my thighs to pull the lace panties I'm wearing—another gift from him—to the side so hard I feel the burn against my skin as they tear.

Before this month, I'd have been shocked, maybe even scared, to know that a hundred-dollar pair of my underwear just got torn apart like cheap dollar store cotton and that I'm helpless beneath the man who did it. Now, though, I feel powerful, wanted, and in need of him to keep going. To take me and fuck me like I'm his, to do whatever he wants to me.

His fingers stroke my folds, gathering the wetness before teasing my clit and making me moan for him. "Pull your left knee up," he growls.

I obey, my strangled pleasure coming out as a gasp as he plunges two fingers inside me. "Gabriel!"

"This is *mine*," he rasps, and I nod, pulling my knee up higher to give him more access. "This pussy is *mine*, this neck is *mine*, these mouth-watering tits are *mine*."

This heart wants to be yours too.

I don't say it, never out loud. Not that I could possibly speak coherently as he pumps his fingers in and out of me, his thumb roughly stroking my clit until I'm left on edge. He holds me here, both of us knowing that he's the one in control.

He releases my throat, and oxygen floods my system as he reaches to his belt, the leather singing against his suit pants as he pulls it out of the belt loops before freeing himself. With one strong, savage thrust he fills me, and even though he doesn't order me, my legs wrap around him, wanting him inside me.

"Gabriel!" I cry out as my first orgasm hits me like a wave

crashing against the shore. He's never, ever denied me my release, not when his cock is inside me. Instead, he rides me through the waves, his hips rising and falling hard and fast. Somehow, he feels me, his strokes matching the crests and dips of my climax, making it even more intense.

"Kiersten," he murmurs, a name that only slips from his lips when we're like this. Not when he's 'training' me or tying me up. Then I'm his pet, his little whore, his plaything.

When he's buried deep inside me, I'm Kiersten. *His* Kiersten.

I let go of the couch to wrap my arms around him, clutching at his back as his pace quickens. He swells, and somehow, I'm still coming from his fingers, the orgasm stretching out until it grows as he explodes within me.

"Mine," he whispers, and I nod, holding onto his neck.

"Yours, Sir."

Gabriel lifts me, keeping me in his lap as he stays inside me, our union intact. "I'm going to ask you something, Kiersten. Something very important. Do you want to stay... like this?"

I nod. "I do, Sir."

Gabriel reaches around, cupping my ass and giving it a squeeze. "I don't do girlfriends. I don't want one."

"I don't want to be your girlfriend, Sir."

"What do you want to be?" he asks. "Answer the question, Kiersten."

"I want to be yours," I reply softly. "I want to be your submissive."

He smiles and lets go of my ass to stroke my back. "Emotions are not something I do."

That's a lie. This man doesn't know the depths he's shown me. In only a month, I've seen so many sides to him. And there's one I cling to.

It may not be love, but he lusts for me. So many times, I've come to him when he's frustrated or angry, when he's exhausted and overwhelmed. And there's always a shift. I would have to be blind not to see it.

He may not say it, and that's okay. He doesn't need to. I can hear it in the softness of his touch, the tenderness of his lips, but also in the hardness of his thrusts and the strength of his hand. I can hear it in the rustle of the dresses he's given me, in the taste of our shared meals.

And I can hear it in the click of the key in the lock when he's had me in the playroom.

But I don't say it. Instead, I hold him, giving myself to him as I roll my hips. "What do you want, Gabriel?"

"Tomorrow, there's another auction. You were invited, were you not?"

"Yes Sir," I whisper as I feel him harden inside me again

"Then you will," he said, pulling my hips in. I start to ride him, losing myself in the feeling of Gabriel's presence and his cock inside me. I'm still so incredibly sensitized. Every rock of his hips is a heaven I didn't know existed before he touched me.

"You're going to get on that stage tomorrow like a good little whore for me."

Chapter 9

Gabriel

The Past, August

My office showcases floor to ceiling windows, a Nineteenth-Century oak desk that has aged better than the finest wines, warm leather chairs, and a private conference table that declares to all that I am the force to be reckoned with. I don't come to you, you come to me.

Rrrring, rrrring.

Sighing, I turn away from my view, seven hundred and fifty feet above the streets of Manhattan.

"Yes?" I growl as I pick up, knowing it's my assistant, Stephens. He's good at what he does, but I'm irritated from being... interrupted. This hour is blocked off for a reason, and this disturbance had better be something fucking important.

"Sir, Mr. Ronald Johnson is here to see you. He says he has an off-books appointment?"

The tension grows in my shoulders as my jaw ticks. Ronald doesn't have an appointment with me, off books or on the books. He's trying to pull a move and salvage what little is going to be left of his pride by the time I'm done with him.

Clearing my throat, I decide it's best to not burn bridges any more than I have to. It is business, after all, and in this world, money changes hands so quickly, it's difficult to keep up. I'll grant him a meeting if it'll ease the tension between us. Only after I take care to hide my task at hand do I answer Stephens. "Send him in."

After all, he lost millions, and I'm the vulture who's swooped in because he *has* to make deals to debt upon debt that's finally caught up to him.

Ron Johnson is the head of the Johnson Financial Group, and while the company is still in the family name, there's no doubt in my mind that he's here to try and keep the company in family control as well.

Greed might be good, but his greed got the better of him.

The knock at the door is stern, and with a brisk "come in", he enters, sharp gray suit, clean shave and newly shined shoes and all.

"Ronald, welcome," I reply, coming around my desk and directing him over to the seating area. With a gentle nod, he greets me and thanks me for seeing him.

I only nod in return, turning my attention to the bar table on the left side of the room.

I offer him a drink. "Whiskey? I've got a new bottle of Port Ellen in that I've been waiting to try."

"Sounds lovely," Ron says, taking a seat. He looks out the window, shaking his head.

"Your company is overextended," I start, cutting to the chase. Some businessmen like to dance around, say nothing but niceties until the rope is fully wrapped around someone's neck before pulling the strings tight.

I'm not that type. I'm more of a stab-in-the-front kind of guy.

Ron knows this. "What can I say?" he says, accepting the crystal tumbler from me when I offer it.

Ron takes a shaky sip, and I feel a bit for him. After the dot-com crash that ironically brought a certain wonderful presence to my life, Ron leaned on his family's real estate holdings to tide the group through. He leveraged and mortgaged over ten thousand square feet of office space that turned out to be a money pit.

"I just need a little to get by this year. I've sold off everything, and the company's back in the black, but cash flow is limited."

I inhale deeply and lean back. "How much?"

"Two hundred million," Ron says. "I know it's a lot, but I also know you're able to make it happen."

I pretend to think about it, even though I already knew my answer before he arrived. "Two hundred million . . . agreed," I reply. "In exchange for two million shares of voting rights stock in Johnson Financial."

"Two million?" Ron asks, gasping lightly. "That's enough to control the board. Even I—"

"Oh, I'd put a rider in the contract. You can buy the shares back," I assure him. "I'm not trying to take over your company. You can keep Johnson Financial for another generation if you want. Or you can find someone else . . ."

Ron swallows and nods. "Fine."

"And," I add, leaning forward, "I want your estate in Scotland. Those shares aren't going to be worth two hundred million when next quarter's financials come out. We both know it. So I want a sweetener, something for me personally. Consider it the interest to the loan."

Ron's fingers tighten on his tumbler, and I know he's debating the wisdom of this maneuver. There are other people he can talk to, banks and such. But if he goes to them, the paperwork will be filed in public.

Ron doesn't want that. He's already made far too many mistakes to allow any more negative press or doubts about the company's financials and endeavors.

"Fine," he relents, and I lift my tumbler. We clink whiskeys and toss them back, closing the deal. After savoring the taste, he swallows and gives me a look. "When?"

"Friday. Send me the account numbers. I expect they'll be numbered accounts in the Caymans or Switzerland?"

"Correct," Ron says, standing up. I stand with him and offer my hand. "They said you drive a hard bargain."

"You'd be just the same if you were in my position," I reply, half-complimenting him. He wouldn't because Ron will never be in my position. But I don't have to twist the blade I've put in his ribs today. Not when I don't have to.

"I probably would. I bet you're a hell of a poker player, Gabriel. In fact, I heard a little rumor. You host poker nights?" My lips tick up slightly in an attempt to find amusement. Adrenaline spikes, and for a moment, I consider him.

I glance at Ron's hand, seeing the groove where a wedding ring used to be. I know the details, of course. His wife divorced him last year. Apparently, she had little faith in his ability to recoup his financial losses. Although there are other rumors as well.

I inhale deeply, rocking back on my heels and slipping my hands into my pockets. "Is that what you heard?" I ask him, curious as to who's been talking. And whether I need to take countermeasures.

My little whore is . . . well, she's mine. What's said about her is a reflection of what's being said about me.

"Something like a game night of sorts," Ron says easily, but I don't relax. I need details.

So I smirk and play it off. "Well, I enjoy a game every now

and then. Would you like me to keep you in the loop?"

The people I play with, I've known for years. I can trust them, or at least I thought I could. I haven't considered inviting anyone else.

But someone talked, and that's concerning. I have dirt on all involved, and they're all a part of the club. We know each other's tastes.

I don't know Ron Johnson's, not for certain, but I know the rumors and how quickly whispers can destroy both reputation and business.

"I would enjoy that," he tells me, smiling and bidding me farewell.

The tension in my shoulders only tightens until the door closes and he's out of my sight.

Pausing to regain my composure, I return to what I was doing before. I go to the door to my private closet, where I open up to find Kiersten, her arms bound lightly behind her. She wanted to experience what's known as *shibari*, or rope tying, and while she's not ready for it . . . I did give her a small taste.

Lunch for me was her exquisite pussy on top of my desk, her legs tied apart in such a way that she couldn't have stopped me even if she wanted to.

"Did you hear that?" I ask her as I slip my hand between her thighs, rubbing her cunt just enough to feel how hot and bothered she is. I left her on edge. She takes a deep breath and nods. "What do you think? Should I have asked for more than his vacation home in Scotland?"

"I don't know, Sir. I'm unsure about the details," she says quietly, squirming lightly. Her lips are parted, and I can practically hear her heart racing. My naïve, sweet submissive. She's smart, wickedly so, but her desire gets the best of her.

Although I'm partly to blame. My poor little whore needed to come before being hidden in a closet with a single light and forced to stay still and quiet.

"I can teach you," I tell her, and her eyes light up. I know she's interested in finance and business. She's experienced in education but not in this world. "You'd like that?"

"Yes Sir," she whispers. When I reach down to cup her chin, her wide eyes peer back at me and her chin lifts. She wants to be kissed and fucked and pleasured. This is her hour, after all, and I've interrupted it.

I smile, petting her hair. "And Ron Johnson? Do you want him to fuck you like the others do?"

She answers honestly, her gaze dropping and then finding mine again. "I don't know. With the masks, I wouldn't know he was even there."

I chuckle before cocking my head. "Tell me something."

"Anything, Sir," she says, whimpering as I reach out and cup her and idly stroke her clit. "Oh, fuck, Sir." As she moans, she falls slightly into my grasp. With her arms still bound, she's unable to stay upright.

"Why do you enjoy that?" I ask. "The poker nights," I clarify as I swallow thickly. I know why I enjoy it and what I think of it all. The others are like toys. They could very easily be vibrators bringing her to the edge, but it's not quite the same for her. I know because we've tried.

"Coming over and over again?" she asks, and I nod. She shivers, her body trembling as she nears another orgasm that's been long denied. "It's a helpless feeling, being tied down and used . . . but it's exhilarating knowing it's not going to stop, and a heady feeling knowing . . ."

"Knowing what?"

"Knowing that I'm yours and you can do whatever you want to me, allow others to fuck me over and over until I'm nothing but a rag doll . . . and you'll still take me to bed, fuck me, and call me yours."

"Because you are mine." My tone is low, even warning. I bend down as I speak, kneeling in front of her with one hand on her throat and the other slipping the thin lace out of my way.

She blushes violently. "I know I am, Sir," she answers with a simper begging to show on her lips.

This woman knows exactly how to touch me, and I'm already rock hard as she looks at me, the silver collar gleaming around her neck. *My collar.*

My Kiersten.

"Why do you like it?" she asks me.

"I don't know," I tell her, inserting a finger into her wet folds. "But the sight of you, from all angles . . . I've never seen anything so addictive in my life. You're right, they want you, but you're taking from them. You get off, you get sensitized, and I enjoy every moan and every expression on your face knowing damn well that by the end of the night, you'll be coming on my dick over and over, unable to stop yourself."

I withdraw my finger, freeing myself and sliding my cock into her and making her gasp. "Sir." Her head falls back. Her arms are still bound, and I help her by moving her legs how I want them, wrapped around me.

"But like a vibrator, they can make you come," I grunt, and she nods. "And I love the look on your satisfied face after coming so much." I thrust again, groaning as she quivers around me and her lips part. She loves sex. But she loves what I do to her more.

I thrust again and bury myself deep inside her, deeper than before, and her lips part into a perfect 'O'. I pretend not to notice.

"Don't get me wrong, your cunt is perfect and tight when I have you first. But after you've been used and every inch of you is sensitive and on edge . . . I can do anything to you and you give me the sweetest moans."

She mewls, her kitten mewl that I yearn for when we're not together, as I thrust again. "Only you, Sir."

I run a thumb along her bottom lip, and she sucks me into

her mouth, sucking tenderly with her teeth scraping against the pad of my thumb. "Right now, though, I just want you."

"You have me, Sir," she says softly, shivering as a mini-orgasm sweeps through her. "However you want." Her perky breasts flush, and her nipples pebble as I pinch them and knead her skin. She's my toy, my pet, my submissive . . . she's *mine*.

Chapter 10

Kiersten

Present

Absently stretching my arms over my head as the dream drifts away, I roll over to a familiar sensation, one that I had fervently hoped I wouldn't feel when Gabriel joined me in bed last night. The chill of the pillow next to me and the silence in the room give it away and jolt me awake.

I'm alone.

Bringing the comforter to my chest, I sit up and listen, but I already know he's not here. Gabriel left. Sadness pricks at the back of my throat as I try to swallow down my disappointment. But, I note as I look at my clock and check the time, I'm not being ignored. In fact, there's a Post-It stuck right next to the clock, and my lips curl on the edges in the semblance of a smile as I recognize his handwriting.

God, I've missed this powerful but narrow, clear script. The bed groans as I lean over, and my hands nearly tremble as I reach out for the note.

You stayed awake all night, didn't you, my Kiersten? Tsk, tsk. I couldn't wake you. I'll be back, and we'll talk. I'll tell you everything I can.

I unstick the note, and after I get ready for work, I tuck it in my purse, re-reading it from time to time as a mix of feelings works its way through me.

I'm taken back to a time before I knew who I was. A time where I trusted him with everything in me. A time when I was only his and nothing more.

And then he left. And I was simply nothing.

I survived, though. This version that survived isn't anything like what I thought I would be. I could have borne waking up alone for the rest of my life if I had never seen him again. But to see him, to feel him, to have him, and then wake up alone?

With a deep breath, I fix my skirt and walk into my office as if this is just any other day, as if emotions aren't riding high and the threat of falling apart isn't overwhelming me.

Time passes, and I accomplish very little, memories coming and going along with doubt and hope in equal measure.

But, I think as I sip my morning coffee in my office, the

note is reassuring. I know, after what happened years ago, he doesn't owe me an explanation. But after last night, I need one. I desperately need to know every detail of what happened after he left.

"You alright, Madam Lynn?" Holden asks from seemingly out of nowhere. He startles me, and I jerk my head up, realizing that I've been staring into my desk drawer at my very special photo. Quickly, I shut the drawer and turn my attention to business. It bangs closed a little too loudly.

"Of course, Holden," I reply, picking up my now lukewarm coffee and taking a sip. "Just fine."

"You sure?" Holden asks, giving me a wary look as he fiddles with his tablet. "You had me a little worried with the text last night. And you didn't answer me this morning. I was about two minutes from rushing over to your place and kicking in the door just in case."

I smile softly and shake my head. Holden's a sweet young man, and very protective. "You worry about me, Holden?"

He holds his hands up, grinning. "Hey now, I'm no white knight. And I know you could take care of yourself if you needed to . . . but I want to make sure you're okay," Holden said before clearing his throat. "You know, being my boss and all."

His little defensive caveat at the end really touches me, and how this kind young man came into my life is something I'll never quite understand but will always appreciate. "Thank you, Holden. And yes, I'm fine."

I'd like to say I'm good, but I'm not sure I'm there just yet. I can't say I'm good until I know what's going to happen with Gabriel and I know the full story of how he could possibly come back. When he left me, I thought it was forever and that he'd never be able to stop running.

And there's almost no chance for things to go back to normal. I'm not the naïve girl from years ago, the girl who started down an unknown path with nothing more than a desire to explore herself and a ton of debt to pay off.

There's too much in my life now to get lost in the touch of a man who could easily disappear from my life overnight again.

Losing him once was difficult. Losing him twice . . . I don't know how I could live.

I can't let myself fall. I can't allow him to ruin what I've made of myself after I had to pick up the pieces alone. I know why it had to happen, but just the fact that it did . . . I thought that meant he was gone forever.

"You sure?" Holden asks again, bringing me back to the present.

"I'm just a little lost in thought right now," I explain. "Uhm, after this, can you have someone make sure the red rooms are up to club standard? I saw the other night that one of the edges was a little jagged."

"Of course," he answers, and as he does, that night years ago comes back like I knew it would.

I spent years with the night terrors reliving that moment. And staring at Holden, different eyes stare back at me, vacant and unmoving.

The blood haunts me to this day.

The body on the floor.

The look in Gabriel's eyes as he looked at me.

The thought makes me shiver, and Holden looks concerned. "I'll stone all the edges myself if you'd like."

"I'd appreciate it," I answer, and I have to clear my throat. It's far too tight, and the emotion is obvious in it.

"I'll take them all up to ten thousand grit stone level," Holden says. "Shouldn't be a problem."

"Good." I can barely answer anything at all as I try to forget it all over again. I shouldn't have come in today. *Gabriel shouldn't have left me alone*, a voice whispers at the back of my mind.

"You sure you're okay?" Holden asks as another silence descends on our conversation. "You look like you've seen a ghost."

"Yes," I answer him more sternly and more harshly than I should as I toy with the necklace at my collar. "Please, don't ask me again."

Chapter 11

Gabriel

The Past, October

The table is laden with chips, over half a million dollars represented in tokens of red, white, and blue.

Not that anyone gives a damn about that. The card game's over, for all intents and purposes, and while at the end of the night, I'm probably going to count out the pile and divvy out the cash simply for form's sake, nobody really gives a fuck about that either.

I won the game tonight, in more ways than one. Not only is my stack of chips bigger than the rest, including capping the night off with a successful bluff to Ron, who had a full house against my pile of nothing, but now I'm hard as fuck watching Kiersten enjoy what she loves on these nights.

Greedily being shared.

"I don't know . . ." Ron pants. He's red-faced and panting as he grips the edge of the bench with all his might to give himself something to hold onto. He finishes after exhaling deeply, "Which is better? Her mouth or her cunt?"

"Let's ask her," I reply, smirking as Kiersten shivers as, from behind, Daniels is doing everything he can to bring her to orgasm. He was one of the last members of my circle of friends to succumb to Kiersten's sinfully sweet temptations. He's also now one of the most eager, and I suspect, one of the most addicted to her.

"So, my little pet," I ask, "which do you prefer?"

Kiersten gasps, her eyes huge as another orgasm sweeps through her. Daniels pauses, savoring the feel of her clenching pussy and letting her ride it out with the feeling of his dick inside her. We all watch, and when it's passed, she smiles, biting her lip. "I love as much pleasure as I'm given, Sir."

"Good answer," Ron replies before I can . . . even though she addressed me. Irritation rattles through me as she turns to go back to sucking his cock.

It doesn't take much to ignore the whispers at the back of my mind while she moans on his cock. I'm rock hard, watching her get what she wants and nothing more than what I've given her.

They're all masked for this encounter. She's not, though.

She never is, and that's always been with purpose. I want to see every little expression she has, every moment in time that she takes pleasure in and any little touches that bring a spark to her eyes. As she comes again from Daniels's cock, her eyes find mine, glowing with vulnerability and submission.

"Oh, fuuuuuck!" Daniels groans out as he can't hold back any further and he finds his release inside her. She's on all fours, and her back arches as she comes with him, her hair falling down her shoulders. She's picture fucking perfect, and I love it, my little whore getting everything she's ever wanted.

He only takes a moment before stepping back for Johnson. He's next in line.

I don't expect Ron to last long, but as he gets into position, he does so almost savagely, driving into Kiersten so hard that her knees slip on the leather and she tumbles. A harsh inhale from her has my spine stiff. Her hip hits the edge of the bench hard, and I know it will bruise instantly. She cries out in pain, her expression crumpling, causing me to leap to my feet.

"Stop!" The word leaves me without thinking twice.

"Gabriel, I—" Johnson attempts an explanation, but I don't give a fuck what he has to say.

"Back up!" I growl, not ready to listen to Ron or his bullshit right now.

I only care about Kiersten, who looks as if she's on the verge of tears. The fuck happened? It was only a moment.

"It was an accident," Johnson attempts to explain from

behind me as Kiersten whimpers. It's more than obvious that she hurt more than her hip.

"Are you alright?" I ask, dropping as many of my guards as I can around these men. I drop to a knee, taking her hand as she lies on the carpeted floor, her face a rictus of pain. With tears in the corner of her eyes, she can only shake her head.

"Red," she whispers.

"That's enough. Night's over. Get the fuck out." I'm harsh, unprofessional, but mostly uncomfortable, and I need them all to fucking leave. She's fucking hurt.

The safe word stops everything. I haven't heard that word leave Kiersten's lips in months, not since the day I gave it to her.

"Get off her," I growl, and when Ron tries to console her, I grab him by the hair, hauling him off her. "That's it! It's over!" My knuckles are white, and the rage inside me boils.

"Fuck this!" Ron yells, getting to his feet. He looks ridiculous, his mask half pulled off, his pants held up by his suspenders while his cock sticks out the front of his pants, but he doesn't care.

"Fucking back off! She safe worded," Daniels, who has an understanding of my lifestyle, says. He's a member of the club. He knows how it is. More importantly, he's the only thing keeping me somewhat steady, heaving in air as my sweet, naïve submissive balls herself up by my feet. He gets in between Ron and me, which saves Ron from having my fist cave in the side of his face. "Look, man, that shuts it down, no matter what."

"Gabriel," she whispers and peers up at me, very much not okay. Her arms wrap around my leg, and just as my hand spears through her hair to tell her it's alright, to let her know they'll be gone in a moment and I can tend to her . . . rage consumes my very being.

"You . . . you've got to be fucking *kidding* me!" Ron bellows, pushing Daniels. I catch him and get in Ron's face, my fist cocked and ready. "She said stop, so we just stop? She's supposed to be your *whore*, for fuck's sake!"

My vision turns to red as I scream at him, only kept grounded by Kiersten holding onto me. "What I call her, and what she and I do, is a relationship that we have. And nothing we do can take away her choice," I growl. "Now leave, and trust me, if you don't, this won't just be your last poker night, it will be your last fucking night on this earth."

Ron gawks, and for an instant I think he's going to give me an excuse to show him what I'm truly fucking capable of.

But instead, he steps back, his face flushed and his eyes full of confusion. "Fucking . . . nothing good ever fucking happens to me. Bullshit like this is why you have to pay for it. I should have fucking known better."

"Time for you to leave, Ron." Daniels is calm, and I'm barely held stable.

"Gabriel," Kiersten whispers as the two men fight. Her gaze catches mine, and she holds me there. Paralyzed and torn, I want nothing more than to kill Ron Johnson.

Chapter 12

Kiersten

The Past, October

It's quiet, too quiet to be left alone with my thoughts. For the first time in almost two months, I don't sleep at Gabriel's palatial penthouse. After what happened earlier today, I just wanted to be alone, but now I'm second-guessing that decision. Gabriel understood when I asked him to go back to my place. I'm still trembling. He drove me himself, dropping me off after walking me up and making sure I was safe.

The last look he gave me is still fresh in my mind, a look of regret and remorse.

As I turn over on my side on the sofa, there's an emptiness and a worry that accompanies me. I'm still sore, and it's not the sweet ache that I'm used to. It fucking hurt. It was only a physical pain, but now I have this unnerving emotional pain, and I can't quite place it, but I know it has everything to do with how Gabriel thinks of me and whether putting distance between us was a wise decision.

Staring at the ceramic mug, no doubt filled with cold tea by now, on the coffee table, all I feel is loneliness.

My apartment's like a stranger's place now, or a photograph of my past. The kitchen is empty, with a light layer of dust on my dishes and on top of my stove. My couch looks dingy, with a couple of dust bunnies peeking out from underneath. From the looks of things, I suspect they've been down there breeding like bunnies tend to do.

But even the mention of the word breeding in my mind sends a fresh wave of throbbing through me. And not the good kind, the kind that comes from Gabriel making my entire body ignite underneath his relentless yet gentle touch. With him, he overwhelms me with pleasure, playing my body like it was made just for him, bringing out the most in me with an almost feather-like stroke.

The other men were only ever… players? Toys themselves? I'm not even sure how to think of them. It was pleasure for pleasure. It was transactional. Never anything more.

My throat dries, and my entire body tenses. I just don't want that anymore, and I don't know how Gabriel will react. I'm bruised and I hurt, and I don't think they could care less.

At least not Johnson, the man who did it. I don't even know who he is. And yet, he hurt me deeply, more than just black and blue flesh. Perhaps it was some fantasy I had in my head that's been brought down to reality, landing with a harsh crash and burning rubble.

Oddly, I feel ashamed that I had to use my safe word, but at the same time, it warms my heart to know that as soon as I did, Gabriel stopped everything. He was willing to fight his friends and associates, rich and powerful men, to bring it all to a halt.

No wonder I feel the way I do about him. But I don't know where we go from here. I don't know what I want or what he wants or . . . all I know is that I'm not okay.

I'm slow as I rise, forcing all the emotion down. My bare feet pad on the floor as I grip the blanket around me. The pain meds are either still working or I'm a fair bit better than earlier. Glancing at the digital clock on the oven, I note it's been four hours now.

Four hours of being alone in a house that doesn't feel like home anymore.

Opening a cabinet in the kitchen, I do see a few items that I've been able to keep over the past few months. There's some peanut butter, which would be great if I had bread, but I've got some crackers next to it that might still be good. And next to it is a box of tea, which sounds just perfect.

Taking all three out, I find my tea kettle and rinse it

out before starting a pot on top of my stove. I take my time grabbing my mug from the living room, and for some reason, I really look at it.

The images on it hit me hard. I got this mug as a Christmas gift my junior year at college, when I'd gone home and Dad included it in my stocking stuffers. It's one of those customizable travel mugs where you can unscrew the whole thing and put pictures or other thin objects between the walls of the mug.

He said it was so that I didn't forget the faces back home. But looking at it now, I'm amazed at how much has changed in the three years since then. How much I've changed.

I doubt my quiet, steady, working class father would even understand. Looking at his face smiling up at me from behind its clear plastic dome, I wonder if he knew even then that the cancer was eating him away inside.

Maybe he didn't care. Mom had been taken from him when I was just two years old, and other than some nostalgic smells, I have no memories of her. Looking at the other photograph, I'm reminded that I do look a lot like her, although it's hard to tell in the mid-eighties' fashion she's wearing while holding baby me.

Dad never recovered from her death. Oh, he smiled, and half of the mug contains pictures of me and him, grinning over everything he tried to give his little girl to make her life complete without a mother.

But when the cancer diagnosis came, it was like he was absolutely fine with it all. Like he was ready and had been ready. There wasn't an option to fight it. It was terminal, so he could have also just been putting on a brave front for me.

In the last four years, everything has changed.

I start the water and recognize that while I might not have my parents any longer, I have good memories of my father.

Gabriel would probably spit on his father if he ever saw him again. His mother . . . well, who the hell knows? She ditched them when Gabriel was still in diapers. His father spent most of Gabriel's childhood either ignoring his son or making ridiculous demands of him, forcing him to act like an adult in a child's body as he showed him off as some sort of . . . I don't know, accessory, maybe? *Here, see the good single father. Isn't his son such a fine young gentleman?*

The stories he's told me late at night when neither of us could sleep are unconscionable.

To say things were tense is an understatement, and from the start of sixth grade until his father died, they only saw each other for about two weeks out of the year as Gabriel was sent to boarding school.

Gabriel didn't even go to his father's funeral. When I asked him why, he said the dead man was a stranger, and the parts he knew of him were nothing he wanted to acknowledge.

Now his only true friend, the only one of the bunch he can trust, is a man named Joshua, who I've met at the club. He's an intimidating man, but Gabriel speaks warmly of Joshua, who I've never met but Gabriel says is 'a handsome sonofabitch.'

I know so much about Gabriel, and at this point, it's impossible to deny what I really feel for him.

Either way, I feel like we were both kind of on our own until we met one another. My college friends have quickly gone their own ways, off to do whatever they've done. I've seen a few emails announcing engagements, and two talking about babies, but none that I feel I can talk to. Certainly not about this predicament I'm in.

My father always did say I was a lone wolf. He prided me on that, but right now, I don't want to be alone. I search my phone thinking of who I could possibly confide in and ask for help.

Hell, in the past six months, I've barely spoken to any of them. The last time I emailed my closest friend, Kelly, was three months ago, responding to her news about her new home in Lugoff, South Carolina. Apparently, Mike, her now husband, was able to get a management position at some chemistry plant there, and with it came a deal on a nice little Colonial-style brick house complete with a garage and a half-acre of land that had three pecan trees on it.

That's it. I have one email from about two months ago, a group email to a bunch of her college friends announcing that she was pregnant, and how is everyone else doing?

I didn't even reply with my updates, although I told them

all congrats. What was I supposed to tell them? That I've spent the past eight months being auctioned off at a sexy club on a monthly basis to be a man's sexual submissive and that's my new "job"? Or that I've had kinkier, naughtier sex than we would even whisper about half-drunk in college? That I know what a saddle, a St. Andrew's Cross, and nylon rope are really for?

What would she say if she knew that my greatest pleasure, at least until tonight, was to get gang-banged until I was nothing more than a ragdoll? Just the thought makes the area between my thighs ache with that painful feeling from earlier.

What would she say if the man I'm head over heels in love with has said time and time again that he's not 'looking for a girlfriend' and that despite that, I'd do anything for him . . . I'd kill for him?

I'm quick to toss my phone down, intent on never picking it back up, as the kettle cries out and I tend to it. After pouring the hot water into my mug and letting the tea bag steep, I head to my bathroom, where I find a bottle of Motrin. Not quite what's hurting, but it's got what I need, and I shake out three pills before going back and taking a sip of tea to swallow it down and then carefully lying down on my couch.

It's only as I sit and hear it groan that I realize this sofa is nearly a decade old.

I could replace this couch. Hell, after these past eight months, I could buy a whole apartment in New York as long as I'm not looking in Manhattan. In Brooklyn or Queens, I could have a decent-sized place and still have enough to be comfortable for a long while. Never in my life did I imagine I'd have this kind of money. Even after the club's cut and taxes and fees, I have over two million in the bank . . . and yet, at this moment, I feel worthless.

If I wanted to leave New York, I could probably find a beautiful house and maybe even retire if I wanted to live cheaply. But I know that I can never fully go back to *normal* life. I can't even imagine a life without Gabriel.

My contract runs out next week. Each of the past eight times that we've done this song and dance, I've known that it was just a game, a contract and a deal. No emotional attachment, nothing but an arrangement.

But will he bid on me again? I grip the mug tighter as more intrusive thoughts enter . . . *do I even want to keep doing this if I'm not getting my other needs met?*

I don't know, but as I sip my tea, I think about every little detail and every possibility. Do I want this life forever? Do I want to be Gabriel's whore, his party favor to hand out to his buddies for amusement? I know it was my idea. I know he allowed it for me . . . but I also know he enjoys it. He's fucking addicted to it now, and I don't know if he'll want to stop. I don't know if it would affect his business relationships.

I don't know anything anymore.

There's a knock on my door that startles me. I can't

imagine who it is. I haven't ordered anything. They knock again, and I sit up, carefully making my way to the door. "Hold on," I call as it comes again. "I'm coming."

I pause at my door, wondering who it might be. A delivery? Gabriel sent things to my place in the past, but since I've practically lived at his apartment full-time, he's been giving them to me directly.

Then again, if he's sending me an apology gift . . . and he's just that sort of gruffly sweet man to do it, too. I pull back the cover on the peephole, praying it's something from him. Like some high-class chocolates, or maybe—

I gasp. I'm a mess, my hair still in tangles from tonight's fucking, and as I smooth my baggy sweater over my body, I can't believe it.

"Open the door please, Kiersten," he says, his voice quiet. "I can hear you on the other side."

Swallowing my fear, I open the door. Tonight is the first time he's ever actually been inside my building. I never thought he'd actually come inside my apartment. "Sir?"

He smiles, lifting an eyebrow. "Are you going to invite me in?" My heart batters in my chest as I stare at him. Expensive suit that clings perfectly to him. Tailored and polished . . . and then there's me.

"Of course," I reply quickly, stepping back and swallowing nervously. *Wasn't I just thinking that this might be my last contract?*

Is he ending things early?

Nervous thoughts scream at me as he takes a step inside and then another. With each step, the old wooden floor groans. Embarrassment heats my cheeks as he glances around my place filled with hand me down mismatched furniture and keepsakes scattered across every surface. One could argue that my decor is eclectic yet comfortable. But right now, all I can think is that it looks nothing like a place he'd ever step foot in.

I close my door after he comes in. My building's cold, and I can already feel a draft around my bare ankles as the door closes and I follow Gabriel into my suddenly too small, too dingy living room.

I have a thousand questions, but he's trained me too well. I keep my mouth shut and my hands in front of me, waiting for him.

"After I dropped you off," he starts, sounding a little less like himself than normal, "I realized that I owe you an apology."

"An apology, Sir?"

Gabriel nods. "We haven't explored it much, but there are couples who are . . . into pain. And one of the most important parts of such a relationship is what's known as aftercare, where the partner giving out the pain cares for and nurtures the partner who's been . . . pushed. Do you understand?"

I nod. "You do give me aftercare."

"Tonight I didn't," Gabriel says, coming over. "Kiersten,

I'm sorry. I should have come up with you and stayed. I should have washed your hair, soothed your aches and pains, and made sure you're okay. I didn't because I was . . . no, I am *still* so angry about what happened."

My throat closes tightly, and with a sting at the back of my eyes, it takes me a moment to respond.

"You're angry with me?"

Outrage flashes in his bright gray-green eyes. "No, hell no! I'm angry I didn't do better for you." As his words sink in, his tone softens and he explains, "I'm angry with myself that I didn't protect you."

"You protected me, Sir," I tell him, speaking out loud without thinking. "Honestly, when I saw you in the hallway . . ." The moment I start, I wish I hadn't.

The words vanish until Gabriel says, "Go on, tell me what you're thinking."

The words rush out of me. "I thought you were here to break up with me and end this between us."

Gabriel blinks as if stunned before reaching out and pulling me close. "No, never. Don't you get it, Kiersten? I'm never, ever letting you go."

Shock keeps me silent until he adds, "Unless . . . you want to leave?"

I shake my head, and Gabriel embraces me, his arms holding me close and warm and safe. I clutch his jacket, inhaling a masculine scent that's uniquely him. Gabriel pulls back. He kisses me tenderly and then lifts me up into his arms and lays me down on the sofa.

"Sir . . . I'm a mess," I whisper, but Gabriel shakes his head.

"If you tell me to stop, I'll stop," he promises me before kissing my lips again.

I nod, and he kisses down my neck, pushing my sweater up to free my breasts. They're not sore at all, and as his lips wrap around my right nipple, I can't help it.

I mewl. Gabriel knows just how to make me feel wanted and cherished, and as his lips and tongue flood my body with desire, I'm floating. This is what I want. More than the money or the jewels or the gifts, I just want him to want me.

I want this man. I need him.

Gabriel's hand strokes up and down my thigh, and when he goes to roam between my legs, I resist for a moment before letting him. I'm stiff, though, and I can't help it. I'm afraid it's going to hurt.

Worried, Gabriel pulls his head back. "Kiersten?"

"I . . . I'm sore, Sir," I admit, and Gabriel nods. Carefully, he helps me off with my pants and then my panties, examining my hips and seeing the bruised spot at the top of my pelvis.

"This happened when you fell off the bench?" he asks, and I nod. "Where else?"

"My . . . my pussy, sir," I admit. "My clit, specifically . . . I think it's bruised or something. I don't know."

Gabriel's face grows concerned, and he softly strokes my

thigh, planting a small kiss on the outside of my leg, sliding off the couch to kneel between my legs. "May I?" he asks. "If there's nothing, we'll go to the doctor in the morning."

I nod, my breath catching in fear and yes, even desire as Gabriel kisses my stomach just below my belly button.

When I go to spread my knees, he stops me, lifting just my right, uninjured leg and propping my foot on the edge of my couch before softly breathing on my pussy.

I pull back, and Gabriel looks at me in concern. "You'll tell me if it hurts."

"I will . . . it's okay, Sir," I whisper, knowing I pulled back out of fear. But I trust Gabriel, and as he lowers his head again, I tremble as he carefully tongues my lips, watching me with intent eyes.

But his touch is electrifying in all the right ways. He knows me so well, and in just a few strokes I'm tugging on his hair, pulling him in to where I want to feel his wet, nimble tongue.

"Yes . . . fuck, Sir, that's so good," I whimper as his tongue finds not the bruised, painful part of my clit but with featherlight strokes, caresses the upper side. I didn't even know it was possible until Gabriel has me squirming, calling out his name and begging for more.

"Oh, fuck," I groan.

"You can come as much as you like, my sweet submissive," he whispers before going back to my pussy and clit. At the same time, he reaches up and strokes my nipples, sending me tumbling over the edge.

Gabriel doesn't stop and instead nurses me through a long, slow, almost sweet orgasm that has my heart swelling even as I come on his tongue.

This is heaven. There are no other words for it. Pleasure takes over. The pain is nothing compared to it. Every bit of aching and worrying for the past few hours vanishes. It's all gone simply because of him.

When waves of pleasure subside and I catch my breath, I look down at him as he smiles up at me. "Better?"

"Much," I reply, smiling back.

Gabriel pulls back and asks, "What else can I do to help you?"

I don't have to think about it . . . but I question saying it out loud. After a single beat of my heart, I ask for something I've never requested. "Will you hold me?"

Gabriel smiles a charming grin. It's not that we never cuddle. The man's an expert big spoon, if I do say so myself. But we cuddle when he wants to, when he feels I need it. But this time, I'm asking, and when he stands up to sit on the couch next to me, I feel a wave of warmth as he pulls me into his arms and we spoon together.

It's safe here in his arms, like nothing can ever go wrong.

"How's this?" he asks as I lay my head on his arm, spooned in front of him on a sofa that's nearly too small. He's got his arm around my waist, his hand resting lightly on my stomach as he squirms a little to get my side cushion just right under his head.

"I like this," I admit, wanting to say more but scared to. I said too much when he was making me climax, and to go down that path now is . . . terrifying. So instead I squirm, intentionally pressing my ass against his groin. "Sir, if you want, I can—"

"Stay right where you are," Gabriel growls softly before kissing my neck. "As much as I appreciate what you're offering, I just want to lie with you for a while. It was a hell of a long day."

I nod, and when Gabriel takes his hand off my tummy for a second to snag the old blanket I've got folded over the back of the couch, I miss his touch immediately.

I never want him to let me go. I don't want anything more than just this.

Chapter 13

Gabriel

Present

Staring down at the dozen roses in the passenger seat of my Lexus, I have to chuckle to myself.

"I'm getting old and soft," I murmur, laying a hand on the wrapper. It crinkles slightly, and the sweet scent of the roses wafts toward me. Maybe it's true. It's an inevitable fact of life that I've probably got more miles behind me than in front of me.

But having her again has me feeling reborn. And when she's in my arms, I'm definitely anything but soft.

Still, twenty years changes a man. When I left town, I was almost penniless. I fled to the UK because I had a few connections there I could trust, and in hiding, with an anonymous identity, I rebuilt. It took me years, but when you know the right people, and more importantly, know where the bodies are sometimes literally buried . . . opportunities are only an ask away.

And I made the most of every single fucking one of them. Part of it, of course, was that my partners were more than content to continue working with me since I would often do the lion's share of the effort while they got to celebrate the public adulation. I wanted to be the man in the background, the shell corporation with a Swiss bank account and little else.

But even an unfair share of billions is enough money that it's now no object to me. My entire life is now dedicated to one purpose and one purpose only . . . *my Kiersten*.

With her in mind, my throat tightens and the anxiousness pricks at the back of my neck. A piece of paper peeks out from underneath the dozen roses. It'd been stuck underneath the windshield wiper on my car when I came out of the florist, and at first I thought it was a parking ticket.

When I pulled the paper out, it wasn't a ticket, and the blood drains from my face once again. Oh, it looked like one, on a parking ticket form and with a logo in the upper left corner that *almost* looked like the shield of the local cops. However, in the box marked *Violation*, none of the pre-printed boxes were checked. Instead, written in the space marked *Other* was a single question.

When did Kiersten become Madam Lynn?

The call to my contact, Roland, was immediate as I looked up at every corner of the lot hoping for a camera. There are none. Whoever left it did so without a trace, but my people are searching for nearby traffic cams and anything and everything that could be helpful.

I'm hesitant as I pick up the roses and get out of my car. If they know her name and they knew my car, then they know where she lives, and she's far safer with me than without me. I fucking hate that this happened. I hate that I did exactly what I feared twenty years ago. As the car door shuts, I nearly slam it, unable to control the swarming regret that's consumed me for hours.

I left her to keep her safe, and the first chance I get to see her, I lead danger right to her. I fucking hate myself. I should have stayed away. Now it's too late, and I'll be damned if I leave her again or force her to start over. She'll hate me. She'll never forgive me.

I look down at my phone again, praying something comes through. Anything at all. I can't imagine who it could be, who could give a fuck, or what they even think they have on me. I'll deny it all. They have no proof. I'll fucking kill them if I have to. I'll do anything not to make the same mistake again.

I'm about halfway through the parking garage and approaching the elevator when my phone rings and I see who it is. "Yes?"

"I was able to get my hands on the nearest security camera footage. It was unhelpful."

"How so?"

"Hooded figure, nondescript clothes, no visible marks or tattoos on the hand. They didn't wear gloves, though. Do you still have the note?"

"It's in my car."

"I could come get it."

I think for a second and nod. "Do it. I don't know if there's fingerprints on it, but do what you can."

"I doubt there's going to be anything, but I'll do my best. Whoever this is . . . they know their business."

"So do I." I hang up and finish crossing the parking lot. Pushing the button on the elevator, I wait, roses in my arms.

I know my business. My business is Kiersten.

And I'm a man who'll do *anything* to make sure my business is protected.

Chapter 14

Kiersten

The Past, December

When this all started nearly a year ago, I never thought it would go this far. I thought I'd maybe have a bit of sex, maybe degrade myself a little bit in the process, which quite frankly turned me on, but also hopefully learn more about what I like and I don't like and make a good amount of money.

I never thought I'd find Gabriel, that he would be my first Dom and my last.

And I never thought I'd fall in love.

I can't deny it anymore . . . I've fallen so damn hard for this man. I can't imagine my life without him. I would do anything for him.

It's obvious to me, and when I look into his eyes, I feel like he's in the same boat with me. It was in the way he cuddled me all night after I was hurt and in the way he's sweetly babied me the past three days.

Even this afternoon, he's babying me. I'm sitting in his office, waiting on him, eager to strip down and climb beneath his desk to give him pleasure however he'd like. Although at this point, I know exactly how he likes it.

It's naughty, and I imagine to my former college friends, the idea of kneeling in the space underneath a man's desk to give him a blowjob would be 'humiliating', 'demeaning', or... perhaps it turns them on too. Maybe they'd find it kinky like I do. Maybe not.

I don't know and I don't give a fuck.

Knowing how much Gabriel wants me is powerful. Knowing that he told me to hold off because he's out getting me 'something nice' to wear for this afternoon and evening. More than likely, it'll be lingerie. Gabriel loves when I wear lacy lingerie. Other than when I'm working out, he wants me in designer pieces from France and Italy. He spends a fortune on it. These boxes come with spritzed tissue paper and delicate pieces he tears easily.

My gaze stays on the office door, waiting for him as patiently as I can, although I'm needier than I've been in months. I've never had patience, and I think he does this to tease me.

Shock sparks through me when there's a knock on the door. I don't say a damn word. It's not my office. Not my place. So I sit as still as can be in his office chair.

Again, there's a knock and I . . . second-guess myself. Thinking maybe he wants to role play? I don't know. It could be him, maybe? Curious, I'm slow to get up and walk over to open the door. The moment I do, I wish I hadn't. My heart pounds as I see a broad-shouldered man in a business suit. He looks . . . semi-familiar.

Swallowing thickly, I greet him, ever conscious of the contrast between his suit and my simple deep red sweater dress. Thankfully, it's not too short. Still, under his gaze, I feel uncomfortable.

"Can I help you?"

The man chuckles, nodding. "Hello, Kiersten. Nice to finally meet you face to face, so to speak."

I tilt my head, immediately on edge. My heart hammers, and I wonder if this man and I have ever engaged in anything. I clear my throat and offer a tight smile, but not overly friendly. One that is kind enough, but not exactly welcoming.

"You have me at an advantage," I press for his name.

"I do," he says cockily and takes a partial step forward. I take a small one back as my heart beats a little harder.

"I'm sorry, are you . . . Joshua?" I know all about Gabe's best friend, but I've never met him.

"No," the man replies, stepping in completely and forcing

me back into the office. "I'm looking for Gabriel."

He pauses in the middle of the office, turning to look me up and down. It's clear after a moment that he's heard about me, and for the first time in a long time, I flush, not with desire but embarrassment.

I know Gabriel calls me his 'whore', but this man's looking at me like I really am one. It's been months since the incident, and ever since then, neither Gabe nor I have been interested in poker nights. I've wondered if it made his associates unhappy, and Gabriel assured me that it hadn't and that they understand. This man, though . . . I just don't like the way he's staring at me. As I back up, my ass hits the desk and my hands instinctively brace myself, gripping its sharp edge.

"I'm sorry, Gabriel's out for a bit," I reply, trying to keep my voice strong. "Mr. . . . ?" My palms turn clammy, and my gaze flicks back to the door, praying Gabriel will stride through it. There's a feeling I can't shake. I don't want to be alone with this man.

I never want to be alone with him.

"Ivan," he says, taking a step toward me. But before he can say anything or move closer, the door opens again and Gabriel comes in.

"Gabriel!" I exclaim, and he glances at me before looking at Ivan in surprise. "Uhm, Mr. Ivan just arrived. He wasn't expecting me to be here." I've never felt such a swell of relief. My hands are nearly shaking.

I just called Gabriel's visitor 'Mr. Ivan' like that's his last name. Not only that, but my tone is pitched and high. It's foolish, I know, but the words escape me before I can stop them. Gabriel doesn't even glance at me, making me laugh nervously. I feel like I'm between two bulls that are about to rush at each other, smashing whatever happens to be in the way.

"Sorry, Ivan . . . Umm, Ivan–"

"That's fine, Kiersten," Gabriel says, keeping his eyes locked on Ivan. "Are you okay?"

"Yes, fine," I reply, stepping to my right toward the windows and out of the way.

Gabriel steps forward, putting himself between me and Ivan, and I immediately feel safer, more secure. "I don't believe we had a meeting scheduled, did we?" he questions Ivan, a slight menace in his connotation.

Ivan squares up with him, and while their fists aren't balled or anything, I can feel the tension cracking through the air. *Who the hell is this man, and what is between him and Gabriel?*

"No, I dropped in for a conversation," Ivan says easily, smirking slightly. "I think you'd like to hear what I have to say. It's important to your interests."

He's cocky, and some of the tension from earlier fades. He's different with Gabriel. That's more than obvious.

Ivan's eyes cut to me and then back to Gabriel, who's gone as tense as steel. Without looking at me, over his shoulder he says, "Kiersten, do you mind waiting in the reception area for me?"

"Of course," I reply. There isn't a part of me that wants to stay here for this. I need fresh air and a moment to gather myself.

"Your package is sitting on the desk in the antechamber," he says by way of saying goodbye, which helps a little as I leave. He's sent me out of the office before for business reasons, but usually into his private bathroom or sitting room.

Waiting in the reception area feels . . . odd. The only reason he would do that is because he doesn't want me to overhear the conversation he's having with the mysterious, seemingly threatening Ivan. That worries and scares me.

The waiting area is quietly busy in that way that city offices seem to always be. Gabriel's role in the firm is a little mysterious, as he seems to operate as an independent personality, someone who has an office for reasons I don't quite understand.

As I peer up from the long sofa at the back of the room, my back to the floor to ceiling windows and a water cooler to my right, I watch the secretaries answering calls and busying themselves. They know me, if only by sight. I don't know any of them, however. Other than purely professional, quick conversations as someone brings paperwork to Gabriel's office, nobody ever talks to me.

It's like they're under orders to ignore Gabriel's kept woman in his office who doesn't have a job at the company.

Shaking out my hands, I wish I'd grabbed my purse so I could have my phone, but I didn't. Although the thought hits me, even if I did, who would I even call? Who would I message?

I don't have anyone at this point, other than Gabriel.

Chapter 15

Gabriel

The Past, December

"Would you like this delivered, Mr. Thompson?"

I look over the pale lavender lingerie, imagining it on Kiersten's smooth skin. I've bought her nearly every color of the rainbow over the past year, and while we both have favorites, for the anniversary of our first auction, and the last one at that, nothing appears to be suitable. There isn't anything that's *enough*. It will have to do for now, but as my thumb brushes along my bottom lip in contemplation, I know I'll keep looking and I'll find something else for her as well.

"No, please have it gift boxed. I'd like to deliver this myself."

"Very good, sir," the attendant replies, carefully picking

up the items and taking them to the back of the boutique.

In the drone of softly playing piano notes, I remind myself, we have a playroom now. It's just for the two of us at the club. It's an expensive proposition, a hundred thousand dollars a year, but with it we can do whatever we want when we visit, and it's just us. We have access to everything, so we can explore her boundaries more.

Because it's going to remain just us, I've decided. I'm sure some would say that I have feelings for Kiersten, and as I hand my credit card over to the attendant, I can privately admit to myself that I do.

But I cannot afford to make it formal. I cannot afford to put a name to it beyond what's already here. An engagement is just a contract. It's a business deal as far as I'm concerned. There are far too many unfortunate lessons in my past for me to allow a contract to come between us.

My mother, who took three million dollars to walk away, abandoning me to a monster masquerading as a father.

A father who didn't want a son and pawned me off on underlings before just shipping me off to boarding school.

I know that Kiersten's different. The way she looks at me tells me that. I could lose it all and she'd stay with me. If the contract were five million dollars or five dollars, she'd be mine.

That's something a man rarely finds in this world.

What we have is perfect as it is. I'm not going to fuck this up with a pen and paper. At that thought, my phone pings, and I half expect it to be her.

It's not, though. It's Joshua. *You could buy her a promise ring?*

I merely grunt at his suggestion before pocketing my phone.

She should officially meet Joshua. He's seen her at the club, of course. He's sat with me during three of the auctions. But they've never met face to face. He's never had the chance to know her. Still, he says she's good for me. Still, he wants me to give in to the social expectations. He suggested that I marry her.

Joshua lost his goddamn mind, although he made the idea somewhat appealing.

And as tempting as that would be, and I admit that it sounds nice, I want to have my cake and to eat it too. I want the benefits without the risk, and while that makes me a greedy bastard, I know that it's not fair to Kiersten to let her think there's more until I'm over whatever hang-ups I might have.

There would be benefits, of course. I could have Kiersten on my arm for real events, not just as 'the girl in my office' or 'the girl in my penthouse'.

My mind reels with all the pros and cons as I'm handed the bag and leave the boutique, taking my time to head back to the car. The brisk breeze is a touch too cold, but I don't rush.

I could have her at corporate events.

I could take her out to fine restaurants, not worrying if the paparazzi might snap a photo.

I could have her at my public birthday party. Not that it's a big event, just a small gathering of my closer acquaintances and Joshua. But everyone will be unmasked, everyone will be recognizable.

Is Kiersten ready for that? Would it shove her away from me?

That risk, that *fear* even . . . I'm man enough to admit that it terrifies me.

Instead, I purchased her something else I know she's always wanted.

It's already at the club, waiting in our new playroom. It's one of a kind, a handcrafted platinum collar. It doesn't resemble a standard collar, though, laying flat across the collarbones and chest in front and nearly an inch and a half wide before arcing up gracefully to a half-inch in the back, where it'll attach just underneath the bottom of her hairline. The individual segments are so finely crafted, so carefully fitted together, that the seams between them are nearly invisible to the naked eye when worn.

In the center is a three-carat diamond, as flawless as the woman who'll wear it. I want that gift to be between just the two of us, in our space, our refuge. I want Kiersten to understand that while I might be too damaged a man to ever be more than her Dom . . . she means everything to me.

It'll be the only thing she wears tonight when I attach her to the playroom's St. Andrew's cross to tease her body however I'd like.

As I drive, with the dull hum of the engine accompanying me, I go over every aspect of tonight.

Of course, kink furniture isn't the only thing in the playroom. I made sure of that, and behind the floor to ceiling partition that runs on a motorized control is a king-sized bed with silk sheets. It is fitted with all the right hidden attachments to allow for any sort of bondage play Kiersten and I might enjoy, but that's not what it'll be used for tonight.

I want to replay our first night.

The memory makes me smile slightly as I drive back to the office, knowing Kiersten is waiting for me there. I hope that my first gift acts as the misdirection that I want it to be, making the second gift all the more exciting and surprising for her.

But when I get upstairs, the receptionist has a tight look on her face. "Sir, a Mr. Lewis came to see you," she says, shifting in her seat uncomfortably. "I told him he needed to wait until you returned, but—"

"It's fine," I reply tersely as I head for my office. Ivan's an intimidating motherfucker, and I'm not surprised the receptionist didn't do anything. But hearing his name puts ice in my blood. If Ivan's here, and Kiersten's waiting for me . . .

yet again. The fucking bastard doesn't know what no means. He doesn't know fucking professionalism.

"Should I call security?" she calls after me as my stride increases.

"No need," I call out.

Their voices are heard through the door as I enter my outer office, gritting my teeth.

My muscles are stiff and tight as I open the door harder than I should only to see Ivan standing too close to Kiersten, reaching for her, and I get in the way.

"Gabriel!" Kiersten says, her eyes wide with emotion. "Uhm, Mr. Ivan just arrived. He wasn't expecting me to be here."

It doesn't escape me that she's scared. It doesn't escape me that she's trying not to be.

My back straightens, every bit of me on edge. "That's fine, Kiersten," I reply, not taking my eyes off Ivan, my tone cold. "Are you okay?"

"Yes, fine," she says, stepping behind me. Inside, I'm enraged, on edge of losing control.

Quickly, I dismiss Kiersten, telling her to wait in the reception area. When she's gone, I lock eyes with Ivan again, my hand balling up and knuckles turning white. "What the fuck do you want?"

"I came to tell you about tomorrow's auction," Ivan says, chuckling. It catches me off guard. There wasn't a doubt in my mind that he was here for business.

Not for her.

"What about the auction?" I lower my voice, hushing it for the secret that the club is, my eyes narrowing.

Ivan's lips tip up in an asymmetric grin as he says, "She's not going to be your woman any longer."

I don't say anything. I don't have enough control to. Without thinking, I charge across the office to grab him by the lapels of his suit and jam him against the desk. It rattles as he slams against it, grunting from the force. With my teeth clenched, I tell him, "She'll always be mine."

Ivan laughs uncomfortably, with his lower back against the edge of my desk. I'm slow to release him as adrenaline courses through me. "He didn't tell me you liked to fight back."

"He?" My jaw ticks, irritation and a lack of patience getting the better of me.

"The one who sent me."

"Who sent you?" I barely get out the words, my throat is so fucking tight.

"Someone you pissed off," Ivan says. With a twist of his hips, he reverses me, grabbing me by the throat. "You're going to lose the auction tomorrow, asshole. He doesn't care if he has to take it to a hundred million dollars. He'll pay it. And if you even try to pull the same shit you did with the first auction . . . someone with less kindness than I have to offer will pay you a visit."

Heat dances along my skin, every possibility racing in the

back of my mind, too quick to process.

"There's not going to be another auction for my Kiersten," I say, eerily calmly.

Ivan's shoulders tense, and his gaze holds a darkness I've not yet seen from him. "That would be a fucking mistake on your part."

"Fuck you," I growl, shoving Ivan toward the door. "She's *mine.*"

"Not after this next auction, she won't be," Ivan says as if it's a statement, but we both know she doesn't have to do a damn thing. As he strides to the door, he adds a comment under his breath. "And then she'll be taught how to *properly* obey."

Rage tears through me. How fucking dare he?

Launching myself from the desk, I tackle Ivan to the floor of my office. My teeth clench as my fist slams into his shoulder, trying to pound the man into the floor. The next punch snaps his head back, landing right on his fucking jaw.

That's going to leave more than a little bruise for this prick. Gripping his lapels, I pull him in close enough to fucking hear what I have to say. "No one is going to lay a hand on her."

When he smiles back, a fear like I've never felt chills me to the bone. Blood fills between his lower teeth. "He doesn't care if you're dead," Ivan says, gripping my hands and pushing me away. "And if she doesn't go to auction . . . he knows her address."

It's then that the door creeps open, slowly, cautiously, and completely at odds with the shriek that fills the room immediately after.

"Gabriel!"

There's an attempt to reply to her. But Ivan's hands around my fucking throat cut it off.

Just as I'm moving to shove him away, to get him the fuck out of here, a loud *clunk* catches me off guard. Suddenly, the pressure on my neck's gone. Ivan sags, rolling off me with a thud on the floor. I slowly rise to see Kiersten standing there with my desk lamp in her hands. It's an older lamp, with a solid brass neck and a weighted base . . . and she just clocked Ivan in the head with it.

My heart slows, everything slows as the reality of what just happens dawns on the two of us. She stares down at him, her eyes widening and her breathing turning heavier and heavier.

"Kiersten?" I murmur gently to get her attention. Her arms shake, and she doesn't look up. She can't turn away. Already, a pool of blood is forming underneath his head on my office carpet. Slowly standing up, I cautiously approach her. Shock and horror are clearly written on her face.

"I . . . I was scared," she whispers, her eyes still locked on the unmoving Ivan. "I . . . I came back to get my phone and . . . and . . ."

"You didn't do anything wrong," I assure her. "Give me

the lamp."

She hands me the lamp, and I can see the dent on the metal base. Kiersten, though, is still looking at Ivan. "Is he . . .?"

"Don't touch him," I order her as she starts to kneel to check on him. "Kiersten, don't."

"But he could be—"

"I know. You need to get out of here," I tell her, and this time it's a command. Reaching into my pocket, I pull out my keys and hand them to her. "Take my car. Go to 66 Perry Street. It's near the corner of 4th and Perry in the West Village. Apartment 12C."

"Gabe?" her voice cracks as tears shine in her eyes.

"Stay there until I come for you," I tell her. "I'm going to fix this."

"Gabriel." My name trembles on her lips.

"It's alright, I'm going to fix this," I assure her, but her eyes reach mine, filled with remorse and regret. "Go," I command her. "Now."

Chapter 16

Kiersten

The Past, December

66 Perry Street. It's near the corner of 4th and Perry. Apartment 12C.

Parking the car, I stare at the building, my hands shaking so hard it takes me two attempts to confirm that yes, the note in my hand and the building number match. Sixty-six Perry Street, near the corner of 4th and Perry in the Village.

It's a nondescript looking brownstone building with weathered white stone on the first floor façade and dark red brick running up the rest of the five floors. The roof's flat, and in front there's a relatively freshly painted wrought iron fence in front of the miniscule rectangle of concrete that's the city's excuse for a 'garden'.

An even dozen steps lead from the sidewalk up to the front door, and with shaky, uncertain strides, I climb them. With each step, I look over my shoulder, certain that at any moment someone's going to stop, point at me, and yell, "Murderer!"

By the time I reach the buzzer by the door, my hands are clammy and my heart is beating so hard I can't hear anything but the rushing of blood in my ears. I feel like I'm about to jump out of my skin. Any second now, I'm going to hear the double *whoop-whoop* of a patrol car, and the first time I try to hit the buzzer button for Apartment 12C, I miss. The second time, the buzzer sounds, and a moment later the lock clicks open without anyone replying.

Apartment 12C is on the third floor, and it takes me a moment of gathering courage before I can knock. My knuckles are white, the skin stretched so tight when I finally do it.

I knock on the door with absolutely no idea who's inside. All I know is that Gabriel told me to come here, and that's enough for this instant. Through the peephole, I see the light go out as someone peers through and the locks click.

"Please come in."

The woman on the other side is in a black dress and a white apron that identify her as house staff. Her feet are clad in black leather, flat-soled shoes, and while she's not wearing anything on her head, she almost looks like a nun.

I wonder if she knows. It's all I can think as she opens the door wider and gestures for me to come inside. My first step is hesitant, but I don't have a choice now, do I?

I glance around nervously as she closes the door behind me, engaging three locks as soon as the latch clicks. "I'm Mrs. Shaw," she says matter-of-factly. "I've been expecting you."

The inside of the apartment is modern urban, with off white walls and hardwood floors that must cost an arm and a leg to rent . . . unless it's bought. Then again, I don't know whose house this is. I just have a sick feeling in my stomach. "Th–thank . . . you."

Mrs. Shaw nods. "Come, I know you are in a state right now," she says. Dread washes over me. She knows. *What does she know?* The questions bombard me, and she seems to answer each as they come.

"I wasn't given details, and I ask that you not share details with me. But I know how to settle the nerves, and Mr. Joshua said that you might have some jangled ones. Here, let's get you comfortable."

Mr. Joshua. It's Gabe's friend. I almost ask if this is his apartment, but I keep my lips shut tight, allowing Mrs. Shaw to lead me wherever she wants. Gratitude hits me for the first time, and tears threaten, but I hold them back.

Mrs. Shaw wraps a comforting arm around my shoulder,

and her grim smile tells me that while this woman might not know all the details, she's well-versed enough in the ways of rich men to know that this isn't a social visit.

After sitting me down on an overstuffed gray sofa, she goes into the kitchen, coming back a minute later with a frothy cup. "Eggnog," she says, handing me the mug. "The thickness will help settle your nerves."

Her smile wavers, and I can feel a wave of pity from the woman. I nod gratefully and accept the mug, sipping at it. It's got plenty of punch to it, and with each sip my brain seems to trick itself a little bit more and more into calming down. Finally, when it's gone, I hand it back to her. "Thank you."

She takes the mug and disappears, coming back with a duster to take care of the mantel over what I assume is a decorative fireplace. It leaves me with nothing to do but stare at the clock that tick, tick, ticks. Bundled in a throw blanket and very much still an emotional wreck, all I can think is that I wish Gabriel would call me. I pull out my phone, but that's quickly put to an end. Seeing me with it in my hand, Mrs. Shaw advises me, "I wouldn't send a text message. Mr. Joshua says that whenever someone uses this apartment, I'm supposed to tell them to sit tight and wait. Reaching out doesn't help with things."

I'm quick to nod and put my phone down on the coffee table. "I don't know what to do," I barely manage to say. My fingers still tremble, and I shove them under my thighs to make them stop. I just wish I could go back. I wish I'd screamed for help or done anything else.

Mrs. Shaw is kind enough to interrupt my thoughts before I can spiral.

"We can watch TV if you'd like. Mr. Joshua has a full cable package available. I do like watching *General Hospital*. It starts in just over half an hour."

Somehow, the image of this prim, put-together woman enjoying the sudsy melodramatic adventures of a daytime soap is just enough to distract me for a moment.

As if reading my mind, she tells me, "Distracting yourself is a good idea right now."

I look toward the door, and Mrs. Shaw shakes her head. "Don't worry, Miss. Mr. Joshua knows how to take care of things. That man helped my family long ago, and even though I'd clean this house for free for him in return, he still pays me double my normal rate I charge my other clients. He's generous but also very, very good."

My voice is low as I ask her, "So you have a secret too?"

Mrs. Shaw chuckles. "Of course. We all have secrets, Miss . . . Now, can I get you a snack?" With her head tilted, she waits for me expectantly.

"I'm not very hungry."

"I think it might be good for you to eat. I think . . . whoever you're waiting for would appreciate your eating?"

I nod, and Mrs. Shaw fixes us a snack, a beautiful

charcuterie board with dried fruits and nuts, a number of cheeses, sliced summer sausage, sliced ham, and an array of crackers. She hums as she goes, and I listen to her, doing everything I can not to think about what happened.

Time ticks on, that clock never stopping. The TV plays, and it turns to white noise in the background. I can't help but look between my phone and the door, my hands gripping the throw blanket to keep me from calling him.

All the while, Mrs. Shaw reminds me that it's alright and for me to simply wait.

Hours pass, and just as fear and dread compete to take over, the buzzer at the entrance buzzes once quickly, then four longer buzzes. "Ah, that's Mr. Joshua," Mrs. Shaw says, standing up and brushing off her apron.

I turn from where I'm sitting so I can see the door, and the moment it opens, every ounce of composure slips. I leap to my feet as Gabriel comes in with a tall, broad-shouldered man. I practically run across the room to embrace him. "Gabriel!"

His scent, his warmth, and his touch are a soothing balm. I murmur, "I'm sorry, I'm so sorry." I've never been so sorry in my entire life.

"Shh . . . it's okay," he says, but his voice is deeply grim. He kisses me on the forehead and releases me to introduce his friend I've heard so much about. "Kiersten, this is Joshua."

"I wish this had happened in happier circumstances," Joshua says, and I recognize the voice from the club. We've only spoken in passing, but still, I've met the man. Never anything else, though. "Has Mrs. Shaw seen to your needs?"

"Mr. Joshua!" Mrs. Shaw feigns a protest, and Joshua gives her a kind look.

"I was just checking, Lynn. I'm certain that you took good care of our guest." Seeing me and Gabriel, he gestures to Mrs. Shaw. "Let us give them a moment."

Reality settles in as they leave, and Gabriel looks at me sadly. "Are you okay?"

"No." I sniffle, fighting back tears. "Gabriel, I . . . I can't . . . I don't know."

"Shh," he says, still sad. "I want you to forget what happened. Don't ever think about it again."

His voice sounds like it just dropped ten degrees, and my eyes widen with disbelief. "What? How?" Just forget? How could I possibly just forget?

"Kiersten, I—"

"Gabriel, we need to talk," Joshua says softly before glancing at me.

Gabriel merely nods and then suggests that I wait for him where I was. I'm slow to take my seat back as they have a hushed conversation. I hear bits of it, and I'm all too aware that I shouldn't be listening. But I do. No matter what Gabriel says, I'll never be able to forget.

"I just got a call from Goldman. He's saying that it'll take some favors, but he can bury it . . . for now."

Gabriel nods and looks at Joshua. "For now?"

"His advice, and I quote, is to not poke at the wound. Let it heal with time . . . maybe."

Chapter 17

Gabriel

The Past, December

The dining room at Paul's Steakhouse is too quiet, with all eyes on me apart from the constant tapping of my thumb on the white-clothed table. The anxiousness that rides through me is very much warranted. Of course, that's usually the case, but this time they're being more surreptitious, more hidden. But I'm a student of behavior, and the more they consciously avert their eyes, the more that I know they're thinking about me.

The question I have is, are they sharks circling the prey, sensing blood in the water? Or are they vultures, looking to swoop in on my already dead carcass?

Because I'm not dead yet. I'm not going down without a

fight. Because if I go down . . . they'll come after Kiersten.

"Gabriel."

I clear my throat and look across the table at Joshua, whose brow arches with concern. "I noticed that we're the center of attention. Not exactly wanted today."

"I suppose not." The adrenaline hasn't waned. My hands nearly tremble knowing what we're here for. I've done a number of selfish, greedy . . . even cruel things in my life. But I've never killed someone. I've never gotten away with murder before . . . and I'm not certain I will now.

While I have enough connections to have Ivan's death left open down at police headquarters without my arrest, that doesn't mean that I'm free and clear. The last thing I want to do is call in a favor. I'd rather handle this as quietly as possible. Rumors will spread. Sacrifices will be made. Which is why I'm meeting with Joshua.

He has connections I don't. Connections that are difficult to come by.

"They all think it was a business deal gone wrong," Joshua says, chuckling darkly. "I suppose that's actually helpful to you, isn't it?"

"In a way," I admit. "It's a secret that stays with us, Joshua. Agreed?"

"Agreed," Joshua says. "Honestly, the assumption is good for both of us. I've been able to burnish my reputation as a fixer, and you . . . well, I assume that your friends across the pond will have heard the whispers. You'll use that to your advantage?"

"In some ways," I admit. "But it's not all to my advantage."

Of course it isn't. I called in a lot of favors to get my new UK passport, and my sudden 'cousin' who needs my presence to take care of them in their permanent illness is hardly authentic.

But it doesn't matter. I will rebuild. It's only a matter of how much I'll have to tear down first. It's been three days. The auction has come and gone, but Ivan's threat and the fact that someone else may be involved haven't escaped me.

There is only one way to protect her when we still don't have the name of the threat that lingers.

"What about Kiersten?" Joshua asks me, and my throat tightens. "What are you going to do with her?"

I swallow, knowing that I hate what I'm about to say. It's torn my soul apart for the past thirty-six hours, knowing that as much as I need Kiersten, as much as I love her . . . I can't have her.

My being in her life would ruin things for her. It very well may get her killed. It's likely. "Until we know who Ivan's contact was, until I know every threat and how all of this will play out, she needs to be safe."

Joshua leans back, uncomfortable. "I looked into it, and as far as I can tell, there was no other contact. He acted alone," Joshua urges, but I don't know that it's true. In my very bones, I don't think Ivan was lying. There was someone else involved. Someone who wants Kiersten, and I've only made matters worse.

"No one came to her apartment," Joshua adds. I told him everything, and Ivan did say if she didn't go to the auction, they would go to her.

He doesn't understand, though. I can't risk a damn thing when it comes to her. So I make the hardest choice . . . and do the right thing. "I'm done with her."

Joshua gives me a look that says he doesn't believe me. "Are you sure? Gabriel, I've never had a true conversation with her, but I see what she's done for you. She made you happy and a better man."

"That may be, but I can't risk it," I reply. "Me leaving? Well, men in our positions have done it before. But to leave with her? She'd be connected to me, and when the hammer falls . . . it would ruin her life."

"Do you think leaving will be easy on her?" Joshua questions. Again, he leans back in his seat, eyeing me. "Your leaving could ruin her too. Ruin yourself as well."

"I know," I admit, although to which part I'm not quite sure. "But this gives her a chance, at least. I'll give her enough money to start over. A new name, a new state. A fresh start without me tainting her life."

Joshua says, "How much are you leaving her?"

"Pennies on the dollar," I admit, the uncomfortable truth

twisting in the pit of my stomach. "Liquidating my assets has been rushed. More than a few bastards are dancing on my proverbial grave right now."

"Those missing pennies bought you your freedom in case something changes here before that case is closed," Joshua reminds me.

Sucking in a breath and forcing my thumb to fucking stay still, I bite out the question that has kept me up at night. "Would you do me a favor? Not professional, no money, just . . . as a friend?"

Joshua nods, guessing my request before I have to ask it. "I'll check in on her. I'll make sure she's safe."

It's the most I can ask for. It's more than I deserve to ask for. "Thank you." For the first time in days, I feel the hint of relief, although it comes with an agony and grief I've never experienced.

Chapter 18

Kiersten

Present

For the first time in years, I'm actually nervous as I unlock the door to Club X. My palms are clammy and my stomach is full of jitters. Then again, most of the time, when I show someone around, they're either an employee who's here to make money or a prospective member. They don't mean a damn thing to me like this man does.

With Gabriel at my side, though, I'm anxious. I hope he loves it. I hope he sees the pieces of us in this place. Maybe by now, he knows, or at least understands, that this is all because of him. Every square inch of Club X was a testament to what he did for me, what he taught me. They're lessons that I've passed on for almost twenty years.

"When did you open this club?" Gabriel asks as we step into the entryway. It's difficult to read him. He brought me flowers and insisted that we come here while the place is closed for him to see what I've been up to.

His energy is slightly off, or at least I think it is. It has been years, and although there are sparks and embers of what used to be, so much time has passed, and we both know our past is covered in ash. Even still, I find myself falling back to the young woman I once was.

"It took me about six months to decide how I wanted each piece to be," I tell him, closing and locking the door behind us. We're alone. It's still far too early for any other staff or members to be here. "It cost more money than I ever imagined."

His steely gaze moves around the room slowly. Rough stubble lines his hardened jaw, and I'm caught staring at him when he glances back at me. A blush creeps up, and I'm reminded of how much power this man has over me. How even after all these years, all I want to do is please him.

As he chuckles, letting his hand brush the small of my back to lead me forward, I distract myself with the details.

"Joshua helped me get it off the ground too, as a silent investor. He worked here for a long time as my security and leading the detail, making sure that the members obeyed the rules. I've learned more than a few things about him through that. I'm glad he's found his wife."

Something flashes across Gabe's expression as I look back at him.

"He met her here," I add, listening to my heels thud across the thick carpet. He follows closely behind, close enough that I can feel his warmth. The heat is on. This far into winter, it takes a good hour for the entire place to be comfortable from the brutal cold outside.

We continue our tour, from the dining and show rooms to the upstairs lounge, where the auctions take place, to the bar.

Gabriel drinks it all in, humming at times when something especially pleases him. "You have my Port Ellen," he notes when we're at the bar and he takes a gander at the available whiskies. "Thirty-one year, even."

"I always make sure to keep that in stock, even if others come in and out of fashion," I reply softly. "It's only available by name request, so we only go through a few bottles a year."

I nearly say *it reminds me of you*. I have reminders of him throughout this place, reminding me of who I really am, but the words stay choked up at the back of my throat. Instead, I slide out a seat and take it, my legs feeling wobblier by the minute.

"Are you alright?" he asks, probably sensing the rise in emotion.

"Gabriel, I . . . it hasn't been easy. I had to change cities, change my name."

"We'll talk later." He cuts me off before I've had a chance to confide in him.

"Gabe, I need . . ." I practically whisper his name as if begging him.

His fingers splay through my hair, cupping the back of my head, his touch instantly calming me, instantly silencing every worry and concern.

"I want to see you how you are now," he tells me, his thumb running back and forth in a soothing motion. "We have time. Let us make the most of this moment." His brow raises as he waits, his gaze never wavering.

With a nod, I agree, and when he releases me, I stand up, smooth my skirt, and push the stool back in.

With my signature red dress and his classic black suit, I lead the way through Club X this time as the woman I've grown into. The version of me that survived what happened all those years ago.

"So, downstairs are the playrooms," I tell him, leading him down the marble steps. "These are actually the newest part of the club. For a long time, this was just a storage area and basement. Members had to meet and could carouse in the lounge or even the auction room. The stage was used for public play, but anything more had to be done in the privacy of people's homes."

"Not everyone can do that, though."

"No, and not everyone has a lifestyle that allows them to bring one or more other people into their homes," I admit. "Some of our group play members were especially tense about it, so with Joshua's help on the contracts and connections, we renovated this entire area into the playrooms and private apartments."

"Private apartments too?" Gabriel asks, and I nod. "Impressive."

"Some of the members joke that with the prices I charge for a month's rent on a private apartment, I'm the one fucking them," I reply with a laugh, and Gabriel laughs along. Our strides are in unison, and with every step, I worry a little less. "Here's one that's currently vacant. Please?"

Gabriel steps inside, taking it all in. I've always liked this room. It's very clean and modern, with just enough hints of color and variation to prevent the atmosphere from being clinically severe or hotel-like.

Approaching the adjustable St. Andrew's cross in the center of the room, Gabriel runs his hand over the sleek, smooth acrylic surface. "I've never been a fan of artificial furniture for play," he says, murmuring to himself. "But I get it. I really like the design, though." A crease forms in the center of his forehead as he adjusts it. "It tilts backward?"

"And the legs can be spread further apart," I add playfully.

He stares at me a moment, but not in the way I anticipated. Not with lust, but with concern.

"And nobody's recognized you in all these years?" Gabriel asks. "You're safe?"

"I am," I reply honestly and with a nod as I lead Gabriel out. There's a tinge of loss as I close the door, as if we should be playing in there, rather than simply carrying on. I anticipate him asking more questions, but he doesn't. He's mostly silent as we complete our tour, past the see-through voyeur's room, the black and metal hardcore room, and more. As we come back upstairs, I turn to him, my heart in my throat. "What do you think?"

Gabriel nods, giving my hand a squeeze. "It's different from the club where I met you, and in a good way. You have more here, more choices. But in the way you've done it, everything is elegant, controlled . . ." I can't help the grin that grows on my face or the way my body warms with his praise. He must know how much he gets to me because he adds with a grin of his own, "You were right. You've crafted a sensual playground that's safer for every member, Dom and sub, than we ever had. I can assume you've had a few bad endings, yes?"

"A few, but so few that I can remember the names and circumstances of each of them," I reply proudly. "I can tell you every single one of them received the outcome they deserved."

Gabriel smirks. "So I've heard."

I smirk back at him, leading the way back to my office. "Joshua?" I guess, glancing over my shoulder, and he nods.

"I know that sometimes I might be too cautious, and Joshua's jokingly said that I mother hen the new submissives, especially those who go up for auction. But if I am, I'm proud of the fact that my wins far outnumber my losses. And the Club's doing well, financially."

"I'm glad."

"There's one more space I want to you to see . . ."

He lets out a hum of contentment, a masculine sound that brings back so many memories. Every nerve ending in my body lights aflame at the sound.

"This way . . . Sir," I tell him, the word slipping out like a lover's caress. Gabriel's eyes glow at the term of respect, and as I take him up the stairs, I feel like I'm showing him the true me. Not my apartment, which he's seen. Not my car. It's just a vehicle.

But as I open the door to my office, I know that my heart's here. This is where Kiersten and Madam Lynn reside together. "This is my office."

As he looks around, my heart hammers in my chest.

This room is where I've spent hours and hours waiting for him to come back for me.

It's in the subtle details, though, that I've poured myself, and as Gabriel's eyes rest on the picture, his lips lift at the corners. "Your collar."

"That's one of them," I point out, going over to my desk drawer and removing the collar with its diamond. "This is the one Joshua said you got for me before you left."

Gabriel's breath catches, and he traces the diamond with a finger. "You did receive it."

"I did."

"Did you ever wear it?" he asks, and there's a vulnerability in the question I haven't seen from him.

"I waited for you to come back . . . to put it on me."

Gabriel clears his throat and steps back, his eyes tightening, and I set the collar back down in the drawer. It's quiet a long moment, and I wonder if he'll allow the conversation to continue from earlier.

"When I learned what you'd done with the money I left you, I have to say I was shocked."

"It's what I know," I explain, and Gabriel nods in understanding. "I wasn't sure I could do anything else at that point . . ." I start but then stop myself.

Gabriel's eyes narrow in curiosity.

"Continue. Explain for me in your words, my love," he says, and in that final word, I feel the knot in my chest loosen. He does still love me.

It takes me a moment to realize he asked me to explain it to him. I'm too caught up on the fact that he called me 'my love'.

Slowly walking to the other side of my desk, I try to bring myself back to that moment . . . but at a safe enough distance. "After you left, I was shattered."

I can't look up at him as I take my own seat. I can hear him take the seat across from me, though. "I cried my eyes out for a day or two, maybe a few weeks, thinking that there was nothing really left for me. But then a thought came to me. When you did come back, because I had convinced myself you would, how would you like me to be? What would you expect of me?"

"You thought I would come back?"

"I knew you would. For years, I waited every day thinking you would simply open that door and tell me how good I'd been for you while you were away."

Saying it out loud makes me feel nearly pathetic. I wouldn't dare lie to him, though. I glance up, brushing under my eyes to keep myself from crying, and catch his gaze.

"At some point, though?" he guesses but doesn't finish the question. He doesn't have to.

"At some point, I did stop waiting, but I still hoped you'd come back."

It's quiet for a moment, so quiet I can hear him swallow.

"And do the Doms remind you of me?" he asks, and I nod. He swallows thickly, his eyes going hooded, and I can almost see him lock his emotions away. "Who was the last man you were with? Before us the other night?"

I blink and realize what he's asking, and for once I have to laugh at my Gabriel. "Gabriel . . . Sir. You are the only man I've ever loved. I never fell for another."

"And yet before, we enjoyed numerous men fucking you," he reminds me. "You enjoyed it. And that's not what I asked."

"Gabriel, I didn't have sex with anyone other than myself and my own personal toys from the moment you had me go to that apartment on Perry Street until the night you showed up back at my place. How could I when all I could think about was whether or not what I was doing would please you?"

"You've never wanted to?"

"More than a handful of times, I've been approached here, in this club. But this is my place of business. And they weren't you."

I finally peer up at him and meet his gaze, a spark igniting there, a flame I know never really went out. His gaze drops for only a moment down to the collar he was never able to give me properly. With purpose, I pick it up and make my way to him.

I lift up my hair, presenting my bare neck, and emotions swell when Gabriel fits the collar around my neck, clicking the catch closed. Lowering it, I look up at him, at the honest emotion showing on his face.

"I could never be with anyone else, Gabriel. I'm yours. I always have been. I always will be." A soft smile graces his lips, although there's still so much to mourn in loss between us. So many years spent without each other.

His fingers slip down my jaw and then down my neck to my collar. To *his* collar around my neck.

"There's a number of things I need to tell you," he murmurs, his gaze traveling down my body, "but right now, I'm going to take off your clothes. I'm going to take my time. And then I'm going to worship your body the way it deserves. I'm going to fuck you against the wall, and then if there's time, against the other wall. If not . . . well, we'll do this tomorrow, and the next day, and the next day, until every surface in your office has felt the touch of our bodies."

He pulls me in, kissing me on the lips with the same forceful tenderness that sets my heart afire. I kiss him back, mewling like his kitten when he takes my hands and places them behind my back. Clasping my wrists together, it all feels so familiar as Gabriel slowly unbuttons my dress, easing the silk off my shoulders to fall back, almost lightly binding my arms together with my clasped wrists the way they are.

"One thing you've kept," he murmurs, laying feather-soft kisses along the line of my throat, "a taste for fine lingerie."

"It reminds me of you," I reply, gasping as Gabriel unhooks my bra and captures my right nipple. *Everything reminds me of him.* He's gentle yet slightly rough, his teeth just barely caressing as he undoes the final button on my dress and lets the material puddle to the floor at my feet. "Gabriel . . ."

"You can say whatever you want," he tells me as he lifts me in his arms, and I gasp, quick to hold onto his strong shoulders. For a moment, I wonder if he's going to carry me to my desk and eat me out like he used to when we would do this in his office. But instead, he carries me to the small loveseat I keep in the corner.

It's just the right size as Gabriel lays me against the white leather, pushing my legs apart. "Hold your knees, my love," he says, and just his new word for me has me eager to obey. Gabriel leans in, kissing my lips before trailing kisses in a straight line down between my breasts and over my stomach to the edge of my panties.

I think he's about to go down on me, but instead, Gabriel tugs my panties to the side and then strokes my clit with such gentle fingers that my head falls back at the first touch. Gabriel knows just how mind altering a feather-light stroke can be. He uses that touch, not a tickle but not a massage, to bring my body to the very edge in just a few minutes.

I moan, and his name on my lips is a plea as I get closer and closer.

"Who do you belong to?" he asks me.

"You, Sir," I breathe the answer.

"Who has your heart?" It beats harder in my chest as he asks me something he never has before.

"You, Sir." Heat floods through me. He doesn't relent.

"Whose heart do you have?"

I only hesitate a moment, and he does the same, pausing his motions. "Yours, Sir," I answer, and he continues. He kisses my inner thigh and runs the tip of his nose down my sensitized skin.

"Do you want to come?"

I nod, biting my lip. "Yes, Sir. But . . ."

"Yes, my love?" Gabriel asks, his fingertip just making contact with my clit and sending fresh waves of pleasure coursing through me.

"I want to come on your cock, Sir. I want . . . I want you inside me." I swallow, knowing what he wants. "Please, Sir. I need you."

Gabriel smiles and leans in, kissing me softly and pushing me back onto the cushions as his hands work at his belt. When he's free, he doesn't even pause, sliding deep into me with one long stroke that has me falling apart and clutching him tightly.

It's heady and overwhelming. His scent, his touch, the strength of his body and how he takes from me. Demands from me. *Loves me.*

Gabriel gives me exactly what I want as he holds me close, pinning me to the loveseat as he strokes in and out of me, our bodies pressed tightly together and our lips sharing breath back and forth.

"Gabriel," I moan as he pumps in and out, my body tightening around him. "Don't leave me."

He promises me, "I'm not leaving ever again."

Past

Joshua sits in the driver's seat of the big SUV, driving almost robotically as Gabriel and I sit in the back seat. He hasn't said anything, giving Gabriel and me some privacy as the car drives down a private road at the airport.

My hands are clammy and nothing feels right. I can't stop thinking about what happened two days ago, and Gabriel's barely told me anything other than that he'll take care of it.

I'm so damn grateful that I'm not in jail, but it's hard for me to ask questions or figure out what to do about any of this. All I know is that I'm responsible for a death and we're now living in a nightmare because of it.

Swallowing thickly, I glance at Gabriel to find him staring out the window. I didn't ask. I only assume he's leaving for a little while.

I want to, but something feels off about this. I just can't shake the feeling that this isn't for a few months. I can't shake the feeling that it's the end.

Tears prick, and I inhale a shuddering breath to keep from losing it.

"Kiersten, it's going to be okay," Gabriel says, his thumb sweeping over the back of my hand. Our hands are clasped together because I can't seem to be able to let him go. "I promise you. You'll be safe while I'm gone."

While he's gone.

"Could I come with you?" I ask him in a whisper.

"It would be better if you weren't with me if anything happens," he answers, and the guilt spreads through me, so I only nod in response and then join him in staring out the window.

It's only when Joshua stops the car on a gravel drive with a small private plane to the left of us that I dare to ask him the one thing that's been on repeat in the back of my mind.

I swallow, looking into his face. He's so distant, like he's already taken off on me. "How long will you be?"

Gabriel gives Joshua a nod, and Joshua leaves us. His door click shut, and the trunk opens with a click. Luggage. Actually, it's a two-person job, and that's part of what scares me. A man who's only going away for a few weeks doesn't pack that much luggage. I could lie to myself and say this is a business trip like usual, but he's taken me with him for those and they've never lasted for more than two weeks.

I repeat my question. "How long will you be away?"

"I don't know how long, but . . ." Gabriel says before his voice catches. He clears his throat, looking past me to the plane. "I don't know."

My heart hammers in my chest, and my stomach clenches. He doesn't know . . . which means it could be forever. I can see it in the way he's struggling to keep his detached demeanor, the way he's lying to me without quite lying. He knows it, and he knows I'm aware of it too.

I'm already on the verge of spiraling. "Don't leave me," I beg with tears pricking the back of my eyes, the words slipping out before I can stop them. I reach out, taking his hand, but this time, his returning grasp is light, barely there. "Gabriel . . . Sir . . ."

Everything in me goes cold, and suddenly, the seatbelt is far too tight. I struggle to unlatch mine as he unlatches his.

"Kiersten, I can't."

I shake my head, desperate. "I love you," I beg, the words tumbling out. "I can fix this. I promise, I'll do anything. I'll be whatever you need, I . . . I . . . we can make it—"

Gabriel turns, his gaze harder, although his eyes can't hide it. "Stop it, Kiersten," he says in a quiet but harsh voice. "I know you want to. But I have to go, and I don't know that I'm coming back."

Tears tumble down my cheeks, and I blink, not wanting to let them fall. "I'm sorry . . . please, Gabriel. Please don't leave me."

Gabriel swallows, and I see moisture in his eyes as well. "You're going to listen to Joshua. It's the last thing I ask of you. He has everything for you. I love you, my sweet submissive, but this is goodbye." And with that, he leaves me there. In the back seat of the car. Shock and disbelief overwhelm me. Every word is stuck at the back of my throat, refusing to be spoken. I'm busy blinking away the tears when the car door shuts.

I didn't even say goodbye. He didn't give me a chance. I

just need a chance to fix this.

I try to slide across the back seat. I attempt to open the door and go after him, but it's locked.

I bang on the window. I scream for him to stop, to please not do this. Tears cloud my vision, and my entire body trembles as I try to get to the front of the private car, but it simply isn't possible.

"No! Gabriel, please!" I've never been sorrier in my life. Never felt more pathetic or alone. He never looks back, and within a minute of him walking up the stairs to the plane, the doors are shut and it moves.

All the while, I'm trapped, watching him leave while Joshua stands to the side, waiting to unlock the car and take me wherever Gabriel told him to.

Chapter 19

Gabriel

Present

"Next, we have Amber," the woman who's acting as the emcee of tonight's auction says as a beautiful woman with flawless brown skin and perky, dark umber-colored nipples, steps into the light. She's gorgeous, clad in a slightly see-through chemise dress that highlights her hourglass figure and contrasts with her skin perfectly.

It's hard to focus on anything knowing I need to tell Kiersten about the note. There's so much I need to tell her. I need more information first, and until I have it, I'm merely living in Kiersten's world, picking up where we left off and learning about the woman she's become and this place she's built in my absence.

I look down at the pamphlet that dictates the night's events, skimming through the information for Amber. She's twenty-three. The color codes by her name say she's experienced bondage and prefers it. She's looking for a Dominant who's an expert in shibari rope tying, and she doesn't want a full-time arrangement.

We never had anything like this at the club where we first met. I was a lucky bastard to have won her. There was no way to know how well we'd fit together.

With the lights dim, I sit back, watching as Amber's bidding begins. She's apparently well-known as a spirited but friendly bidding war starts up between three members, unknown men in masks who slowly bring the price up to three-quarters of a million dollars before one, a man with a tinge of gray at his temples behind his almost ridiculously undersized domino mask, makes the final bid and wins. He's clearly elated with his purchase, though, his charming smile broadcasting everything to the entire room.

Why wear such a small mask when every other man in this room can more than likely ascertain who you are underneath it? Well, I suppose that when Club X rules require a mask but you don't want one, you go with as small or revealing a mask as possible.

Joshua's already given me a rundown of men who come here and who exactly they are. Just as I ran my business,

Kiersten runs the club, knowing every dirty and dark secret of the men we do business with. Just in case it's required. Drinks are served as the lights on the stage dim for a moment and they prepare for the next bid.

I scan the room, looking for anyone who may be out of place, but Joshua's convinced that whoever placed that note isn't a member, and every man here is accounted for.

With the lights brightening, there's a rustling in the room as the men sit up straighter. The next woman approaches the center of the stage, a little more hesitant, her fingers playing at the hem of her chemise. I have to wonder, how would my Kiersten walk onto the stage now? After all these years, as the woman she is now. Would she still stride as if she sees no one, yet stare into the audience searching for me?

I know, in watching her interact with the members as Madam Lynn, just how much she's desired by so many of the members, both men and women. Would she still look for me in the crowd?

I've certainly noticed how a number of members stare at her collar. A part of me very much wants to publicly claim her, to declare to all of these men that Madam Lynn, the woman who makes all of Club X happen, is *mine.* It's not like I don't have the money, honestly.

The other part, though, is resistant to claim her, thinking back over what Kiersten's done for the past two decades. I always gave her the option to pursue outside projects when we were together. Despite my nickname for her, she was never just a 'whore' to me. And if for a moment I thought she truly believed that's all she was, I would have banished that word from my vocabulary.

But to know that she's spent her youth working, driven by what we shared for those precious months, shames me. She did it all alone. She did it all while mourning and with false hope. I should have been here with her.

We could have explored, played, had years of passion and growth together.

We could have had those years.

We've lost so much time. Time that we'll never get back. And I'm the one who made that call.

"Your whiskey, sir," a waitress says quietly, approaching. She and the other staff are the only people in the room who aren't wearing club membership bracelets, and that thought reminds me of my own fresh bracelet on my wrist.

"Thank you," I respond gruffly, accepting the drink. Even with security detailing us since the moment the note was found, at a distance so Kiersten isn't aware, I don't intend to drink. I only ordered to fit in with the crowd.

I take the glass, swirling the amber fluid around in the tumbler. Like the years slipping past us, the alcohol spins around, leaving nothing behind in its wake. But like the alcohol itself, it can devastate the body and heart.

A chill ripples down my spine, and I can feel the hairs

on the back of my neck rise up. I set my glass down, looking around the room. Someone's watching me.

I turn around to see no one there. My gaze moves across the room, searching for the stare that gives me the chills of knowing someone is watching.

There's no one, though. No one is looking at me. All of the Doms are focused on the brunette on stage.

There's a lot of subtle posturing going on in the room, men who clearly know who each other are despite the masks and who are playing similar games to what I used to do long ago.

So of course, a few of them are curious about the new mask in the group. They obviously want to know who I am and whether I represent a new challenge to the games they play. If only they knew how very uninterested I am in anyone other than Kiersten.

The chill runs down my spine, but it's none of them. Their eyes might glance over me, but once they see that I'm not bidding on a particular woman, I'm at least temporarily dismissed from their minds.

I can't see anyone when I turn around in my seat again, yet that feeling won't go away. I remind myself that this place is the most secure building I have access to at the moment. Joshua and his men have surrounded this place, and there's nothing at all I can do but wait. I message Joshua just to alert him in case anything is amiss. A man in a suit enters shortly after, security for the club, but he leaves within minutes.

There's nothing. There's no one.

I watch the room, ignoring the women and ignoring my fantasy of winning and claiming Kiersten publicly again. There's only one thing on my mind—find the threat and end the threat. Silently and permanently.

Because I won't let what happened before happen again.

Chapter 20

Kiersten

Present

"I don't like it."

In some ways, it's imploring. Holden sits across from me in my office, digesting the revelation I made to him about Gabriel. I've glossed over most of the details, of course. But I had to confide in someone, and Holden saw Gabriel in the club, he saw the collar on my neck, and he asked. So I told him. I let it pour out of me. He's a man from my past, and not only do I vouch for him, but Joshua vouches for him as well. And we're involved.

"There's just something . . ." He licks his bottom lip as he shakes his head. "I don't like it."

My nerves prickle, and although I appreciate the protectiveness, it's irritating. He thinks he can have a say in who I'm involved with?

"Why is that, Holden?" I ask. "If you want, I can point him out on the cameras. He's not doing anything wrong or breaking any rules."

Although we were getting rather naughty just a few hours ago. I don't have cameras in the office, though, thank goodness.

"It's not that. I'm just saying . . . this guy just waltzes back in and you're fine with it?"

"There's a lot of reasons he left," I confide a little more. "Holden, I loved him. I've always loved him. He's the man who inspired me to become the woman I am today. And he cares for me." Instinctively, my fingers reach up to brush the collar, and Holden's gaze drops before his brow furrows.

"If he loves you so much," Holden counters, "why the hell was he a fucking ghost for twenty years?" Hearing the way his voice rises, Holden holds up a hand, taking a deep breath and calming himself. "Sorry, Madam Lynn. But it's more than just my job to worry about you. He could be out for your money. Have you thought of that?"

Before I can respond, he presses further. "Is he the one who scared you the other night?"

I let out a huff but also let it all roll off my shoulders. He's young. He has issues with trust because of his family. He doesn't know what happened, and he'll deal with it.

I'm warmed by his concern, but this is one time where Holden's natural suspicions are misguided. "Holden, I know him. I know your job is to be wary of everyone who enters those doors. And I know that you have good instincts. But Gabriel is more than just a businessman walking in and wanting a membership."

"So why was he gone for so long?"

I sigh, standing up. I've made my decision, and I need to end this. "Something happened in my past. He protected me."

"Something . . . he was protecting you because you did something," Holden says as if he understands. As if he's starting to get it.

For a split second, a small blip of a moment, I want to spill it all to him. It took years to get over what I did. The remorse from that grave incident mixed with the loneliness and the worthlessness I felt nearly brought me to a darkness I could never return from. I still remember the sound. I still have nightmares every once in a long while. I've never forgotten. No matter how much I try to forgive myself, I'll always be a murderer.

I've never told a soul, not even Joshua who knows me from those days. I suspect Joshua knows the truth, but we've never discussed it. And after all these years, unburdening my guilt feels safe now, like the last little piece to finally let go.

But I won't because that would hurt Gabriel, and no one ever really needs to know. Even a young man who doesn't understand and has had issues with trust all his life. He doesn't do secrets, and I understand that, but this isn't business. It's personal.

So instead, I cross the room, trying to end the discussion. "You could say something like that, Holden."

Holden backs up to the door, standing between it and me. As if he would dare block me from leaving. My brow cocks. I'm more than certain my expression reads, *as if you would dare*. In response, his gaze drops a moment in shame.

"Holden, I've made my decision. I appreciate your concerns, but this will not help your argument. Now get out of my way, drop your concerns about Gabriel, and let's get back to work. The auction should be ending soon, and there are documents to have signed."

The Holden I know returns, looking if anything a little chagrined. "I'm sorry," he says quickly, almost stammering. "I'm sorry, Madam Lynn. I just . . . I'm really worried, that's all. I get a really bad feeling about him."

I pat him on the shoulder, trying to heal this rift that's suddenly popped up between us. "I understand, but you don't know him, Holden. You'll get to it, though. You'll warm up to him."

Holden hums and lifts an eyebrow, muttering beneath his breath as he leaves, and it leaves a chill to run down my spine that I do everything I can to ignore. "It's been twenty years. Are you sure you know him?"

Chapter 21

Gabriel

Present

"Gabe, old man, how are you?"

I lean back in my chair, chuckling. "I'm not as old as you, Donovan. What's on your mind?"

My priority is maintaining a low profile. Privacy comes at a price, and with that price is usually a decent amount of luxury.

Like this place I purchased for the moment. Spacious, the two thousand square feet are a lot for a single man in a house. But the almost suburban three-bedroom ranch house is very comforting, with dark leather chairs and a modern dining room and kitchen.

The second bedroom was converted into a temporary office. It's low-profile from the outside, however it's still furnished to my liking. It's the quality Donovan expects.

Outside the house, Joshua's team is still active, but low-profile and at a distance. There's far more security at her place and at the club.

In the back of my mind, I'm always thinking about Kiersten and whether everything will be alright now that I'm back. Legally, I'm protected. The case is closed, and there isn't an ounce of evidence. The nervousness of knowing someone else is aware that I'm back and knows all about Kiersten never leaves me.

But business never stops either, and as Joshua suggested, I need to play the part. Whoever is watching will slip up, and we will find them and deal with them. Until then, the show goes on. And Kiersten is none the wiser.

Donovan and I have been business partners for nearly thirty years. As the scion of an old, noble family, Donovan learned a hard truth about the modern aristocracy in the UK and Europe when he grew up.

Titles don't mean shit compared to what they used to.

So while Donovan's hereditary title might have opened some doors for him at Rugby and Cambridge, it didn't do a damn thing compared to what really gets the influence in the modern world—money.

For that, he turned to me. In a lot of ways, it's been an

ideal situation. As a noble, he's able to be the public face of our partnership, soaking up the tabloid adulation and massaging the public perception of our moves. And he's good at it. Affable, he can go from appearing like a sharp businessman to your folksy uncle next door with just a change of clothes and a bit of hair gel. Either way, his accent is always endearing, and he has a charisma that can't be taught.

Meanwhile, I work in his shadow, turning millions to billions with deals and trades and partnerships where I am never a face or a name. I have my privacy, he has his praise and fame, and we both earn wealth beyond imagine.

"Well now, I received another message from our friends," he says, and my expression tightens ever so slightly. I resist rolling my eyes and merely gesture for him to continue. I understand the need to keep secrets. I have my own, after all. But Donovan's not important enough to worry about the NSA or MI5 or whoever may attempt to tap into our already encrypted video chats. Yet he still insists on not naming names sometimes and speaking in code. "They're still very interested in the Wentwood Towers."

As I lean back, the leather wingback chair groans. He waits for my response as I take in his comment.

The Wentwood Towers was one of my first business arrangements when I arrived in the UK. It's an older skyrise. Nineteen years ago, it was one of those addresses that had prestige, that carried with it an unspoken endorsement of you or your business.

If you said that your flat or your business was in the Wentwood Towers, it meant you were *someone.*

But times have started to change. Not that the Wentwood hasn't been updated. It has. It's still prime real estate. But with the rapid pace of new building and renovation occurring in London, the Wentwood's value has peaked. Honestly, I was only holding onto it because the mortgage was already paid off and it's nearly all profit at this point. And it lends Donovan some of that traditionalist aura that all British nobles are supposed to have. You can be modern, but not *too* modern.

"Are they ready to talk?" I ask.

"I think so," he responds.

"If the numbers are right, then let's talk. If not, then we tell them to bring back some numbers that make sense."

"That's what you're supposed to do, remember? They want to meet in person," Donovan says. "I guess what I'm saying is, when are you going to get your arse back over there?"

It's a good question. The truth is, I've avoided this entire region of the United States for twenty years and have only been back in the States on limited occasions for a reason. I don't need any of my former associates recognizing me. I only do in-person meets when necessary. So when business has pulled me back here, it's always been to the other side of the country.

But now . . . "Donovan, you know I have business here

as well, and I'm not sure a real estate brokerage requires me to attend."

"Of course," Donovan says, "but you have billions of pound sterling and euros of business back in the UK as well. Things that I cannot handle alone and need your presence for."

I take a deep breath, nodding. Donovan's right, of course. And when I came back here to see Kiersten, I left without knowing what the future held. So I didn't burn any bridges back in the UK, and they're clearly expecting me. The mere thought of Kiersten brings back a nervousness that's unsettling. Some businesses are far more pressing than selling a property.

"Send me the details and I'll look it over," I tell Donovan. "I've got something to handle right now. If they're serious and require an in-person with me, they'll wait."

"Is there anything I can help with? Or anything I should be concerned about?" he asks, and my jaw ticks, but I keep a smile firmly in place.

"Not at the moment, but you know I'll let you know if any enticing offers come up." I blatantly ignore his second question, and that doesn't go unnoticed by Donovan, who peers down for a moment before lifting his glass of whiskey for another swallow.

With that, the business side of our talk is over. Donovan is less than pleased but now more firmly aware of where I stand at the moment.

Conversation is easy until the hour is done and I walk him to the door.

It's only when the door closes that I can let out a breath I've been holding. I don't move an inch before checking my phone for any update at all. And there's nothing other than his confirmation that everything and everyone are in place. Nothing to report and nothing to concern ourselves with.

Whoever left that note could have simply been fucking with me. Someone who resents me, and that list is a mile long. Someone who heard a rumor and wanted to get to me. Someone who wants me out of their territory. Whoever the fuck it is, I will find them, but it may take time, and I've never had the virtue they call patience.

Slipping my phone back into my pocket, I go to the dining room of my new house, preparing. I knew I had to take this meeting, but I've prepared for tonight for Kiersten.

The table is set with a fine white cloth, with a sterling silver candelabra and high-end place settings.

The setting is perfect, and when the soft knock comes from the door, I dim the lights. Opening the door, my breath is taken away as Kiersten stands on the other side, utterly beautiful and elegant in a long-sleeved, ruched dark red dress that clings to her curves. My gaze immediately drops to her chest where the deep V reveals more than enough.

"Gabriel."

"You look beautiful tonight," I greet her, holding out a hand.

"It's a little more revealing than I'm used to," she admits with a grin and a slight blush. I love how I can still make her blush. Every worry relaxes as she takes my hand, letting me lead her inside and to the dining room, where soft music plays and our chef-prepared dinners now wait underneath gleaming steel domes.

"What's this?" she asks, her eyes widened with surprise and her dark red lips pulling into a bright smile as she turns to me. I suppose she thought I wouldn't spoil her. She should know better than that.

"I thought we could have a night, just us," I reply easily.

"Hmm," she answers playfully and with a softness I remember so well, looking around. Spying the wine on the table, she lifts an eyebrow. "Looks like you're trying to romance me." There's a way she carries herself that entrances me. It always has. I don't know what it is, but she's intoxicating to me.

The way she seems so at home in a place she's never been. The way she doesn't hide her wants and her gratitude. And that smile she gives me when she peeks up at me after spotting the notebook at the edge of the table.

I meant for that to be given after dinner. Maybe after a drink. I could use liquid courage to confess what I've done.

"You can pick it up . . . it's yours." My tone is less authoritative than I'd like. I've never had anyone to share my past with or my vulnerabilities until Kiersten. And when I no longer had her, it killed me.

It's a leather-bound tome that I bound myself before coming back to see her. Kiersten opens the cover, glancing at the first page. "What's this?" Her dark red lips purse slightly as the candlelight leaves shadows to dance across her face.

"I missed you when we were apart," I explain as she turns the page, looking at my handwriting. "I wrote letters. Every Sunday. I knew I couldn't mail them to you, but I wrote. They're twenty years of my thoughts, my dreams, my wishes for you and of you. Yes, I wanted to romance you tonight, Kiersten. But I need you to know that I never stopped wanting you in my life. Still . . . my only wish in life is to have you, my Kiersten, in my life. I have never stopped loving you."

She's quiet as she reads the first page, and I'm not exactly sure she heard me until she peers up, her eyes glassy as she whispers that she loves me.

Chapter 22

Kiersten

Present

The silk wrap around my wrists binds me to the bed, and I squirm, gasping as Gabriel drags the whip over my nipples. "You know," Gabriel muses as he looks down at me, a grin on his lips, "There's so much we still haven't done."

"S-Sir?" I ask, trembling as the whip traces over my stomach. There's the occasional smack against my thighs. Tapping against my clit. He uses the tools to toy with my body and light every nerve ending along my body on fire with anticipation. He's already made me lose count of the number of orgasms I've had. Every little touch sends me closer to the edge now. Every breath is heavy, and I want nothing more than for him to take me.

I didn't anticipate tonight going like this.

Tied down to his bed, wanting to please him, needing him to take me. For years I've hardened, for years I've tried to move on. And in a single night, every piece of me is his again.

The bed groans when he leans over me, his naked body brushing against mine. His erection slips against my heated core, yet he doesn't enter me, no matter how much I beg. His breath is warm as he murmurs, "There is so much I could do to you right now to get you off."

He brings the whip to between my legs, the soft leather floating against my clit. I'm already hypersensitive, but Gabriel knows me so well. Leaning in, he kisses me as another orgasm sweeps through me, swallowing my moans. I'm still quaking as Gabriel gets between my legs and slides inside me, hissing as my clenching walls grip him.

Oh my God. My head falls back in unadulterated pleasure.

"I love how you feel wrapped around my cock," Gabriel whispers as he pulls back, thrusting into me again.

The truth is, I'm falling . . . no, I've fallen in love with Gabriel again. Wholly and completely. With every thrust of his cock inside me, I feel myself slipping over the edge, tumbling further and further into a world where I'm Kiersten again, not Madam Lynn.

It would destroy me if he ever left me again.

"Kiersten," Gabriel grunts in between deep, powerful

thrusts. "Look at me."

I open my eyes, gazing up into his handsome face as he takes me like I've always been his. The burning fire in his eyes warms me, tells me that he's the same way.

"Gabriel," I whisper, wishing I was untied so I could clutch him. Instead, I wrap my legs around his waist, drawing me in deeper with each stroke. "Gabriel . . . Gabriel . . ."

"Kiersten, I—" Gabriel starts, but a sharp *crash* splits through the room. Gabriel covers me, his arms around my upper body, and as he stills, a scream leaves me in terror.

What the hell just happened? A cool breeze blows over us, and other than my heavy breathing, I can only hear the tinkling of glass.

"The window?" I ask, my heart racing. I'm brought down from the highest of highs immediately. Gabriel's phone vibrates on the nightstand as he unbinds my wrists.

"Are you okay?" Gabriel asks first, snatching the other end of the bow knot holding my wrists together and releasing me. Concern is etched on his face.

"I'm fine . . . but your window . . . Broken glass," I reply, my eyes finding the curtain that's now fluttering in the wind. "What . . . watch yourself."

Gabriel nods, getting off the bed and slipping his shoes on to walk carefully over to something on the carpet. He squats down, picking up a rock.

His expression is stern, and again, his phone goes off. It's faint and I almost didn't hear it. I wonder if it's been going off the entire time.

"What is it?" I ask, reaching over and grabbing a sheet, holding it to my chest as the chill flows into the room. I can't help but feel like a damsel in distress, lying naked in bed with a sheet clutched to my chest like a string of pearls. It's ridiculous, but at the same time, I can't deny that I'm scared.

"What is it?" I repeat, and Gabriel only glances at me before going to get his phone.

He knows something. Anger threatens as I realize he means to keep this from me.

"Tell me right now, what's going on?" His eyes lock with mine, and he only hesitates a fraction of a second.

"There's a note," Gabriel says, taking a piece of paper off the rock. Carefully, he unfolds it, reading aloud. "I know what you did. You never should have come back. Leave her alone."

My blood chills. "It's a threat?" I can barely get the words out, my throat is so tight. I've had issues in the past, but never a fucking brick thrown through my window. No one even knows where I live.

"From who?"

"I don't know." He's straightforward, and I nearly ask him who's messaged him when he picks up his phone, but he tells me it's Joshua and that he's already on it.

"What the hell?" I ask, swallowing my heart. "Gabriel, call the police."

"No," he says, folding the note up and putting it on the dresser. "No cops."

"Gabriel, I—"

"Kiersten, this isn't connected to the club or to Madam Lynn. This is connected to our past," Gabriel says. Then he asks me a question that fills me with dread. "It has to be. Who did you tell about Ivan?"

He stares back at me as if I'd ever tell a soul.

I swallow thickly, needing to clear my throat before I answer. "Ivan?" I ask, and even twenty years later, a chill goes down my spine at the mention of that man's name. "No one."

His expression is grim as he gathers the pieces of glass from the floor.

"Gabriel . . . who did you tell?" I ask. "Who did you tell about Ivan?"

Gabriel rubs at his cheek, his voice catching. "Everyone." He goes to the window, looking out into the black night. "Twenty years ago, I let them all believe that I killed him."

Chapter 23

Gabriel

Present

"The grounds are clear," Roland says as he comes into the living room, the lower part of his black pants slightly damp with the late night frost. "Nobody around, the whole neighborhood's quiet." Roland is Joshua's right-hand man, and he's been my contact since I've been back. Joshua is following the tracks on foot with three men. The rest stayed behind.

"Thank you, Roland," I reply, adjusting the shirt I have on. I'm underdressed, in just jeans and a hooded sweatshirt, but right now I have to be able to move quickly. On the other side of the living room, Kiersten sits on the sofa, huddled in the clothes I found for her, shivering with shock and worry. This is exactly why I didn't want to tell her.

"Do you have the footage?"

"Here," Roland says, handing me a memory card. "I already looked, but there's nothing identifiable."

"Like before," I muse, and Roland nods. "Understood."

"I'll go keep watch outside," Roland says, making his exit. In the silence, I toy with the data card between my fingers and then slip it into the slot on my laptop.

"What did you mean, like before?" Kiersten asks. When I don't answer, she repeats herself. "Gabriel. What did you mean when you told that man, like before?"

"There was another attempt to . . . frighten or message me," I explain offhandedly as I pull up the data. While I wish I could have set up security cameras all over the neighborhood that fed directly to my computer, the best I could pull off was cameras that weren't obtrusive and could be hidden around the neighborhood.

"What do you mean?" she presses, leaning forward. My Henley on her is baggy and makes her appear small and fragile. I know she's anything but. She's not naïve. But she's mine to protect, and I wanted to fix this before ever speaking a word of it. "Gabriel," she raises her voice, but her tone is one of a plea.

I relent. "They stuck a note under my windshield."

She gasps, and I know there are a million questions running through her mind.

"I had both Roland and Joshua investigate," I continue,

advancing the video. There are four cameras, all of them synchronized to the same time stamp. "It was part of the reason I picked this property instead of another city central apartment. I thought by having one of my shell corps purchase this place, We'd have had privacy and security. Apparently not."

I almost tell her about the men on the perimeter. How I deliberately asked for privacy tonight. How Joshua messaged first before advancing on the man in the hood after he snuck in on a motorbike from the back. He was closer and faster than the men on foot. All because I was naive enough to think that I'd taken enough precautions.

A brick through a window, though? Through the bedroom window, at that. *How did he know? How could he have possibly fucking known?*

The video starts, but it's like what Roland described before. A man, average height, average build, wearing nondescript clothes and a hoodie. None of the angles catch a glimpse of his face, and I doubt that they'd be able to see anything even if they could. The man wore gloves, not like before.

I highly suspect his face is somehow also obscured.

"Jesus," Kiersten whispers, looking over my shoulder. I hadn't even realized she was there. "That's all?" Her small hand lands on my shoulder, and I take a moment to cover hers with mine. She's in only a Henley as she leans slightly over the armrest of the chair, the lit fireplace behind her cracking and hissing. The light casts shadows across her face, highlighting the concern. I want nothing more than to make it all go away so I could take her on this sofa, right here and now, and promise I'll protect her. Time. I only need time.

With a heavy inhale, I turn back to the cameras.

"That's all we had last time," I admit, closing the video as the man runs into the night shadows.

"I just got chills," she murmurs, and her arms cross in front of her as she holds herself. "A few days ago . . . I felt like someone was watching me," she says almost as if to herself. "And then you showed up, and I figured it was only you."

My blood turns cold at her admission. I call out for Roland, and in an instant, he appears.

"What do you need?" He's far more casual than Joshua, yet also far more serious. Perhaps that's because I've known Joshua for longer. He's the only man on this fucked up Earth I can truly call my friend.

"Get me every bit of surveillance you have on Kiersten over the past two weeks," I tell him. "I want a list. Every person she's talked to, every person she's been in contact with, everything."

"You—"

"Someone's stalking you," I continue forcefully, looking Kiersten in the eyes. "And I'm going to find out who. There's no way that I will let you be in danger, Kiersten. So until we find this asshole, you won't go back to your home without me, not back to Club X without me. You're not leaving my side."

Kiersten stares at me, her eyes wide and full of shock. "Are you kidding?" she asks, anger brimming in her voice. "You want me to put my life on pause because—"

"Kiersten, I'm looking out for you," I protest, stressing the very real potential threat.

Her voice is strong, yet it still shakes. "I've been on my own for years, and if—"

Standing up, the laptop falls to the sofa, and I grip her chin in my hand, meeting her gaze. "I refuse to lose you. I won't let them hurt you."

"You don't even know who it is, Gabriel," she whispers, taking a step back. The pain in her eyes is evident. "You didn't even tell me." Her focus moves to the fire as the deception and reality hit her.

She paces the floor, twisting her hands behind her back. "You *knew* that there were issues. You *knew* that someone was making threatening gestures, and you didn't *tell* me?"

It's silent a moment, deathly silent apart from the fire that rages behind her. Adrenaline pumps hard in my veins, and I know I could have told her. I could have showed up, fucked her, and then the very next day informed her that I'd brought danger to her front door. My throat tightens. "This isn't how I planned it. I didn't want to keep anything from you. It simply didn't seem necessary."

Outrage flashes across her beautiful eyes, and a part of me fucking loves the fight in her. The independence. But I'll be damned if I worry her more than I need to. I'll be damned if put her in danger for the sake of her being strong on her own.

"I'm not letting you out of my sight."

Kiersten shakes her head. "Gabriel, whoever it is, I have my own—"

I step forward, closing the distance between us. We're close, like any minute she could slap me or we could fall to the floor making love again. I don't really know which. I just know that she's *mine.* "Kiersten, I'd rather die than let you leave my sight again."

She's silent, but her expression says it all. How it softens, how the flash in her eyes is of something else now. Something we had long ago.

"I want you to know, I'll allow security because I'm not a damn idiot," she tells me and swallows thickly, her gaze never leaving mine. "But I'm damn pissed that you kept this from me. I'm going to need a little space and a little time."

The back of my teeth clench as I bite down on every emotion and thought that screams in my head. "As long as you are with me or my team, you can have as much space and time as you need." Just as she objects, I cut her off, unwilling to negotiate or discuss it further.

"You're mine, Kiersten," I tell her. "You can be pissed at

me, but you're still mine, and I'm going to do everything I can to protect you."

Hours later, in the middle of the night

"I need . . . space," Kiersten murmurs, and I knew it was coming. It's all too much, and the fragile memory of what we once had can only burn for so long before it's snuffed out. In my silence, she adds, "I need to think."

Part of me wants to deny her, to tell her that she's not leaving my sight. But I would rather give her what she needs than force her by my side.

I nod and point toward the back, maintaining a calm exterior. "The bedroom on the left across from the main is made up for sleeping. The other is being used by Roland and his men as an office, but you can have privacy there."

"No cameras?" she asks, and I shake my head, trying not to smile. "Promise?"

"I don't need film of you to remember how beautiful you are," I tell her simply, and Kiersten stops in the doorway, looking back at me. There's the spark, the flame that burns dimly in the chaos. I see it in her eyes. I hear it in the silence.

Time passes, and I know she feels it too. Even if I've fucked up.

"Every day without you was torture," she says softly.

With that, she leaves, and I try to think through things as I wait for Roland and Joshua to finish their sweep. There's nothing else for me to do other than watch the videos again and again and again, searching for some clue that I've maybe missed before.

Hours pass through the late night, and there's nothing there. Not a damn thing that's helpful. When Roland comes in, I'm already exhausted, frustrated, and fucking pissed. The sun peeks over the horizon, and while that might be only slightly late for Kiersten after running Club X for years, I'm still not quite adjusted, let alone able to sleep. "What did you find?" I ask Roland as he stands in the doorway, a grim look on his face.

"The neighborhood's been swept twice. Full crew on duty." He runs a hand over the back of his neck. Lack of sleep darkens his eyes.

I can only nod in understanding before clearing my throat and thanking him for the update.

"I'm at the door," Roland says. "Unless you want me somewhere else."

With nothing to go on and exhaustion weighing me down, I decide sleep may be needed, although I have no idea how I'd be able to with the ruminating thoughts of what will happen when we find him, or worse, if this man gets what it is that he wants.

I can't help myself . . . I listen in at Kiersten's door. Just to check on her. Just to know she's alright. The creak of the bed alerts me to tossing and turning. Slowly, I open the door.

The queen-sized bed is made up with a flannel sheet and comforter set from a big box retailer, and the walls are a plain pale blue. I suspect that the former owner used this as a kid's room. As she lies on her side on the bed and her heavy breathing raises her shoulders, all I can think is that this room is certainly not fit for a woman like her.

"Kiersten?" I whisper, but she gives me the cold shoulder, turning over and staring at the far wall. Sighing, I come over and sit on the edge of the bed. "I fucked up, I know. I should have told you about the threat. I was just . . . it's been twenty years, and I just got you back. I didn't want to risk things."

"But you did risk it," Kiersten says quietly.

"I know. I'm sorry."

"So, what now?"

I shrug, reaching out but not laying a hand on her comforter covered body. "I'm hoping we can move on. Not forget, but learn and move forward."

"It can't be like it was twenty years ago," Kiersten says, turning over. "We're not those people any longer."

"You're just as beautiful."

Kiersten shakes her head. "You need glasses, it seems."

"What can I do right now to help you?" I ask, lowering my hand to touch her. "Do you still need space?"

She's quiet a long time before she turns over to finally look at me. "Do you think the past is catching up to me?" she asks, tears pricking her eyes. "Like, long lost karma?"

I slowly shake my head in reply, keeping her gaze. It fucking kills me that the fear is so evident in her. "I'm the only thing from your past that caught up to you, my sweet submissive. Don't think about that."

She parts her lips to say something but then stops. I know she thinks it's only empty reassurances. I can't make it all go away that easily. The look in her eye is the reason I didn't want to tell her, but there's no way I'm going to say it. I don't want to fight anymore.

"I can't sleep," she repeats, and I feel ashamed. I never wanted this for her. Never.

"Can I just lay with you and hold you?" I offer. "Just that."

Kiersten nods and wipes away a tear that I didn't see in the dim bedroom light. "Please."

I kick off my shoes and slide under the comforter, wrapping my arm around her from behind. I kiss her shoulder, inhaling her warmth.

"It's going to be okay," I whisper into the shell of her ear. Her only response is to hold onto me tighter. I didn't realize how much I needed that until this very moment. I hold her until she's breathing softly, finally on the path to sleep.

I've got a long way to go, though, for sleep to find me. Because the fact is, we didn't find the man who's set out to threaten us.

Whoever it is, the man is a ghost.

Chapter 24

Kiersten

Present

I repress a sigh as the black-suited man with me hurries ahead to check the room before I can enter. It's been days, and each day is worse than the last. I barely slept the night before last. Yesterday, I slept on and off throughout the day, keeping to myself in a guest room of Gabriel's while he and Joshua tracked down a lead to nothing. I understand his wanting to protect me, so he can understand my cold shoulder when it comes to keeping vital information from me.

"Hughes," I start, "We're inside the club. You don't need to check every room every single time." Robert Hughes is a nice enough man, but I'm exhausted and everything about this is

. . . it's too much. There isn't a chance in hell that anyone inside these walls is a threat.

"Madam Lynn," he says, not agreeing or disagreeing with me. At least he used my preferred name for the club. It's maddening, and pretty much the only response he makes. I've known him for years. He was hired by Joshua, so I know he's a well-trained professional.

But I despise this Secret Service treatment. It's not what the club needs. If word got out to members that there was something to be concerned about . . . it could cause irreparable damage.

I informed the staff that I was sick yesterday, but with security in and out . . . I don't think they bought it.

Nervousness pricks its way through me. Perhaps this was a mistake.

"Thank you," I reply with a sigh, proceeding on. I know I'm angry, but it's a displaced anger. I'm not mad at security, certainly not Hughes. He's been accommodating, all things considered. I'm not mad at Joshua or Holden or any of my staff.

I'm mad at Gabriel. Hurt more than angry. I fell in love with him, head over heels like the naïve woman I used to be. And the entire time, he was keeping a secret from me. How could he have been genuine with me if he wasn't even being honest?

Perhaps I'm hardened and skeptical. Perhaps the pain

from the last time lingers more than I realized. I'm not sure. . . . but right now, I need a little space. Maybe more than just a little.

Work is just that. But time passes slowly, and I can't focus on anything. Emails pour in from employees, and members as well, asking if I'm alright.

Fuck.

I haven't felt this helpless since . . . The realization threatens to bring up emotions and memories I'd rather not deal with. With a deep breath in and a slow breath out, I do everything I can to simply keep myself steady.

My phone pings with a message. It's from Gabriel. *I love you.*

Scrolling back, the last few days he's messaged every few hours to tell me just that.

We're safe.

Everything's going to be alright.

And *I love you.*

I message back, reluctantly because I'm still angry, but I can't not respond to him.

I love you too.

I start with a cup of tea that I spend far too long stirring before checking the inventory numbers.

Although I find myself staring at the screen, unable to focus and think straight. Every few minutes, I realize I'm still on page one, and I've been thinking of something else. Of the moments that used to haunt me and moments I thought I'd long forgotten.

A knock at my door saves me from myself, and I shake off the tension in my hands, setting my tea aside. "Come in."

"Madam Lynn," Holden greets me, coming in and closing the door behind him. "How are you?"

"Missing a lot of mental balance, but I'm surviving," I reply honestly. Picking up my tea again, I take a sip.

Before he can get a word in, I set the tea cup down with a clink and ask him directly, "So, is everyone talking behind my back?"

"You're the Madam," Holden points out. "Last week, you were on cloud nine. You'd walk down the hallway, and the carpets wouldn't even have marks from your heels in them. The past few days, though, you look like you've got weights strapped to your ankles and invisible thousand-pound weights on your shoulders. Now, I know some of it . . . but the others don't. They're worried about you, that's all."

"They're not supposed to be worried about the boss," I murmur at the realization that I'm failing them. I shouldn't have come back. Gabriel was right. I'm far too bitter to admit it to him, though.

"You're the boss, yes. But you're also the head of whatever you want to call this secret little conclave, like the head of a family. And when Mom's troubled, all us kids worry about her."

"So I'm Mom now?" I crack a smile for the first time in

days, a bit of warmth flowing through me.

"I mean, you know." He gestures, seemingly embarrassed for a moment, and I let out a short huff of a laugh. "So, talk to me. It'll help, I promise."

I lean back, wondering if he's right. I've done the same thing with so many of the young subs here at Club X, and sometimes, just saying things helps. I couldn't possibly tell him everything. But the pain I feel, knowing Gabriel kept a secret from me the very moment he came back . . . I just wish I could stop it. I know it's tied to the past. I don't know how to just be right now. It feels as if I'm spiraling all over again.

"I feel like my heart's broken in two," I admit, reaching out and sipping my tea. "I love him, Holden. Okay? I'll say it. I love him deeply. And yeah, I yelled at him, I gave him the cold shoulder. That doesn't change that I love him."

"What happened?" he asks.

I hesitate a moment. "Secrets," is all I say, and he waits for more before nodding in understanding.

"So you love him . . . But?"

"But I hate the fact that ever since he came back into my life, everything's turned to absolute chaos," I add. "He came back and with it . . . it brought everything back. I'm not willing to go backward, Holden."

"Why?" he asks, leaning forward.

The sleeplessness from last night weighs on me.

"Hey." His voice is comforting. "Let me make you another

cup of tea, and maybe you can just rest today."

"I don't need a day off." I start to protest as a yawn interrupts. *Dammit.*

"You don't need to leave. There's a sofa right there." He gestures.

I glance at the sofa, knowing not even a week ago, Gabriel and I shared it and a piece of my heart slipped back into place.

"Hey, what's wrong?" Holden asks, and I realize my expression is far too honest. "You can tell me."

"I can't, though," I confess. "Years ago, I did something awful. And Gabriel covered for me. I owe him my life, and I love him, but I just—"

"He covered for you?" Holden asks, a mar in his forehead.

I can only nod, confessing, "He did everything for me, but he left me. His coming back is like hitting play on a pause button for a movie I never wanted to know the ending of." Holden listens, nodding along, and as the tears stream down my face, I hold everything I can in and I don't say another word. I've already said too much.

"Let me get you another tea," Holden offers, not judging and not pushing further.

"Thank you." I pluck the tissues out, and the moment the door shuts, I admit to myself what I've been denying for three days straight. I'm terrified.

If someone knows, they either want Gabriel dead . . . or they want me dead.

Chapter 25

Gabriel

Present

"And this is all you have?" I ask him to make sure.

"Yeah," the shop owner says, pocketing the envelope I just passed him. There's five thousand dollars inside, and I seriously doubt he's going to be reporting that to the IRS. "Look." The owner finally looks at me. His white button-down shirt is ironed, and he's paired it with blue jeans. No tie, not that I would expect him to be wearing one. "I don't have the most up to date system. The memory card's set up to record on a loop, like a DVR. If I don't pull the card, it auto deletes anything more than five days old. The dude I paid to install this thing called it a security spam folder." He shrugs.

"Sorry I can't do more." Like the other shop owners on this corner, the man is older and the place is a bit rundown. Not much has been updated on this strip.

It's more than likely another dead end. Still, I pocket the card. It's something. And anything is better than nothing. "I understand." We've gone through hours of footage from three dozen security cameras, tracking the hooded man until we reach a dead end. This camera may have a view, it may not, but it's worth a look. And to the man behind the counter, that's worth five grand.

"Have a good day," he tells me, and I respond with a curt smile and "You too."

I leave the shop, a compact shoe store that's half a block down from Kiersten's apartment, and head down the street. This was the third place I've been to today, helping Roland and my team gather as much information as we can on who's been leaving these threats.

It's been three fucking days. Three days too many of not putting an end to this goddamn nightmare. Three days of Kiersten barely speaking to me because I kept it from her. I know I fucked up, but I'm going to fix it. Then, I'm going to fix things between Kiersten and myself.

At the corner, I'm met by my driver for today, another man from Joshua's security firm. Joshua's watching footage and current surveillance. Together, we walk to my vehicle for today, a black detailed SUV that's far more secure than the soccer-mom look it's sporting. "Were you able to find what you need, sir?"

"Doubtful," I tell him, pulling out the memory card and adding it to the pile.

When we get into the SUV, he plugs it into the built-in computer and with a few keystrokes sends it on its way to the rest of the security team. "Don't worry, sir. If there's anything there, they'll find it."

Although I know he's right, relief is hard to come by.

I nod, leaning back in the padded leather seat as the driver takes off.

For the hundredth time today, my mind wanders to Kiersten. I know she's safe, but I hate not being right by her side. Space and time are two things we've had for too long.

She's all I think about as the engine rumbles and I wait for a call from anyone. An update on any fucking thing. I've only been back for a week, and yet it's like we've picked right back up to where we were.

No one calls during the drive, and there's no update when I return to the office.

I sit down and open up a video chat to my security team, needing to get an update on anything. Fucking something. "What have you found?"

"Still nothing, sir," Roland says. "We've seen three potential sightings of the stalker on the footage, but nothing concrete."

"What do you mean, potential?"

"Male, average height and build," Roland explains. "There are a lot of people to narrow down, but we're doing our best. He has always kept his face unrecognizable or hidden from any cameras. I even had the techs try to do the whole 'reflected image enhancement' thing. Which, by the way, is ninety-eight percent bullshit compared to what you might think it is from television and movies."

The knot in my stomach tightens. "So no leads?"

Roland shakes his head. "No. We're still analyzing the newest footage, but I'll be honest, Gabriel, this might be a waiting game. He'll fuck up at some point. Nobody's perfect forever."

I nod, leaning back. "Understood. Do your thing."

Roland clicks off, and I sigh, trying to think and make a list of names that Joshua doesn't already have. Alone in the study, all I can do is go over every name I've ever known.

When I left, he spent years cleaning up the mess, so to speak. Everyone assumed it was an altercation over business and a supposed accident, although rumors spread that it was malicious. Every whisper was dealt with. Blackmail is a useful tool, but it's not one that's foolproof or one that's effective forever.

Joshua's tracked down every name on the list, finding their locations, verifying where they've been for the last week. Every single one is accounted for, every associate who had any idea of what happened that night seventeen years ago.

Who the fuck could be coming after me? Not that I don't

have enemies that have been freshly made, but Roland and the team have already accounted for nearly all of them. Most are still overseas and nowhere near the East Coast.

I wouldn't have come back if I thought this could happen.

A knock shakes me from my thoughts. It's a dull echo from the front door, and there's no message on my phone.

Anyone who's able to knock on my door has either already been cleared by my security team, or my security team's dead in the hallway.

I peep through the fisheye lens, and within seconds I have the door open as an old, familiar face stands on the other side.

"Joshua," I greet him cautiously.

"Gabriel," Joshua says, stepping inside without invitation. Joshua's always been a little cold when on a task, a little bit detached from the rest of the world. It's not that the man doesn't feel. I know he does.

He just knows how to divide his life into compartments. And business is business.

As soon as the door closes, he turns, smiling a little. "How are you doing?"

"You can guess. Is this good news or . . . ?"

"No leads, but I wanted to check in with you." His hand rests on my shoulder, and I realize this isn't about the threat.

We embrace, brotherly, clapping each other on the back hard before turning and heading into the living room. "Want a drink?"

"Not until tonight," Joshua says, shaking his head. "I've got family duties."

It's almost shocking to think of Joshua as a family man. When we were young, he was the man who we knew of as a fixer. You had problems . . . he fixed them. For a price, of course. But he earned every cent, and I can only guess at what secrets are filed away in the back of his mind.

Now, while he's still imposing, almost uniform in his dark suit, there's hints of gray at his temples, and the ring on his finger is worn, slightly dulled from age and the minor scratches that gold always picks up unless it's polished regularly.

"Good . . . I'm not feeling like a drink either," I admit, sitting down in the corner chair of the living room. Looking Joshua over, I feel unfamiliar nostalgia sweep through me. "It's been too long."

"It has," Joshua says, unbuttoning his suit jacket and leaning back on the couch, crossing his legs.

"How's Kiersten?" he asks, and I shake my head, looking toward the doorway. "She's pissed, she's upset, she's a wreck."

He gives a nod of understanding and then one of sympathy.

"I'm worried for her," I admit.

"She's alright. My team is with her."

"No . . . I'm . . ." I clear my throat. "I'm worried about finding out who it is and then how she's going to be after. I remember what you told me about her when I left."

Joshua leans forward, shaking his head. "It's grief. It comes and it goes. She's strong."

"She is." I nod, knowing she's every bit the woman I loved back then, but more.

"Kiersten is as close as family to me. Hell, she introduced me to my wife. So we're going to figure out who the fuck this is and get rid of him."

"I keep thinking over the messages," I tell Joshua, trying to move on before the feelings rise up again. "Trying to connect them somehow to Ivan, or maybe Ron Johnson."

"Not Johnson," Joshua says. "He's dead."

"Dead?" I ask, surprised. "When did that happen?"

"Two years ago," Joshua says. "The loan you gave him, and had to forgive, by the way, might have kept his business afloat. But it wasn't a panacea for a man whose time had passed him by. Seven years after you left, he was voted off the board and his kid took over. He 'retired', dropped off the radar for the most part until he died. My sources say he drank himself to death."

"Let me guess, his funeral was well attended, and there were nothing but dry eyes in the house?" I ask, and Joshua nods. "How long until that's my fate?"

"Hopefully, it's not going to happen," Joshua says. "I've seen how your coming back has affected Lynn . . . Kiersten. Whatever. I've also seen how this fight between you two has her broken up inside. Now, I'm not intervening, but I'm also going to do my best to keep the road between you two smoothed over."

"Should that road even exist at all, though, Joshua? What if . . . what if someone knows and is coming after me through Kiersten?"

"No way," Joshua says. "Gabriel, if it were any other man in the world saying that, I'd take it as an insult. From you, it's just a worry. There's no evidence. I destroyed it all, and anyone who might know anything is either dead or has done worse shit by now."

"Worse?"

Joshua chuckles darkly. "You and Kiersten . . . you two deserve each other."

For a moment, I feel a bit of relief. Just the thought of the two of us being together again, of spending what's left of my life with her . . . Subconsciously, I check my phone again. No messages, and the dread comes right back.

"No news yet," he informs me. "We'll find something."

"If we had a name, it would be faster."

"I told you there was no reason you couldn't come back. Whoever this is . . . they can threaten all they'd like, but they don't have shit on you," he reassures me, but I don't buy it.

"So what the hell is going on, then?" I ask, reining in my frustration. "If nobody can touch me, if everything is taken care of and all the years that I spent away from her were supposed to bury this deeper than the fucking Titanic . . . who the fuck is doing all this?"

"Gabriel, she's safe," Joshua reminds me. "We're going to find him."

As if on cue, his phone pings and then pings again.

He answers with, "Yeah?" and then he's quick to stand, and every muscle tightens as he puts the phone on speaker.

Roland speaks on the other end. "We have a partial and two more from the shoe shop footage. We started with the night you got the note, and we have a hit on facial recognition."

"Send it now."

"I don't have to. Sir . . . It's Holden."

Everything slows down at this moment. Time ceases as it hits me. Holden. He was here all along. "It can't be" are the first words from Joshua, stunned and in disbelief.

"We had three images pulled. All three matched."

"I have two men assigned to Kiersten. Holden is one of them," Joshua says with urgency, his face going white. "Get down there now!"

I'm quick to text Kiersten, *Where are you?*

Kiersten! Where are you?

All the while, panic and chaos stay on the edge of my periphery. I nearly type that he's a threat, but I don't want him to know that we know. I struggle to know what to message, so I call her while Joshua barks orders. No answer. I call again. No answer.

With the order given, Joshua dials someone else quickly,

pressing it to his ear. When there's no reply, he tries a different number, and then a third. "Yeah . . . where's Holden and where's Madam Lynn? What the fuck do you mean, you're not at your station? . . . Well, *get there*. And find them. *Now.*"

Fear races through me from his tone and the urgency as I grab my keys and head out, not waiting for the explanation, although he gives it to me.

"Holden separated the internal security team," Joshua says. "Said that there was a suspicious person outside."

The only thing I can think is that he's hurt her. I have no fucking idea who Holden is or how he knows anything about her past unless she told him. Fear runs rampant in every move I make as we rush to the car.

"I swear to God—"

"I know," he says. "Trust me, if he hurts her, you won't need to. I'll fucking kill him myself beforehand."

Chapter 26

Kiersten

Present

When I wake up, the first sensation I have is one of motion. It's weird that you can sense that sort of thing, even when you're not accelerating or decelerating. But there's this unmistakable feeling to riding in a car that just says, *you're in a car.*

But . . . how? Why? And why am I lying horizontally? I make a move to sit up, but my head whirls like I'm going to pass out.

I try to open my eyes, but there's something over them. It takes me a moment to realize that I'm blindfolded, with only a dim light sort of coming through the weave of whatever cloth has been tied around my eyes.

My heart pounds at the realization. Fear cripples me.

Slowly and quietly, with my heart racing, I try to figure out what the hell is going on. My wrists are tied together in front of me, but I can move my arms. A blindfold that I could very well remove, but the moment I think to do it, a voice chills me to my bones.

"Don't try and reach for the blindfold," Holden says from in front of me, and it steals my breath. A slight bump at about my waist confirms for me that I'm in a car, and I'm probably laid across the rear seats. My heart races as panic sets in.

Holden? My voice is caught in my throat. *What happened?*

"You know, one of the nice side perks about working for you for these last couple of years . . . I've learned all sorts of little skills." His tone is menacing, not at all like the Holden I know. My throat dries, and I struggle to believe this is real. It must be a nightmare.

"Like those bondage displays and lessons that the club has all the time. It's almost comical how easy it is to loop the wrists to the neck to make sure you stay right where you are. I'd have done your ankles too . . . but I'm no monster."

"Holden, what are you doing?" I ask in nearly a whisper, swallowing my fear.

Holden replies with a dark chuckle. "Stay quiet. We're almost where we can talk."

Tears leak from the corners of my eyes as reality sets

in. Does Joshua know? Does Gabriel? Questions and fear bombard me to the point that I almost can't breathe.

All I can do is try not to panic. Although I'm on the edge of failing that task.

"Holden?" I question, again wishing this was only a terror in my dreams.

"Shut up." His cold, unfeeling response guts me. It takes me a moment, maybe a long time, I don't even know. But I breathe and I attempt to make sense of anything I can.

I listen, trying to gather whatever information I can to figure out where we are. But Holden's car is soundproofed very well, and I can't hear anything outside the soft rush of the engine and tires on pavement.

When we come to a stop and Holden shuts off the car, my pulse races and the panic of the unknown rages inside me.

With the car off and the silence setting in, he cuts through it before I gather the courage to speak.

"What do you want to ask me? One question."

"Are you . . . the stalker?" I ask, trying to remain calm. "The one who threw the rock?"

"And the one who left the note under Gabriel's windshield wiper," Holden confirms. "Come on, time to get out."

Fear is palpable, and my limbs go stiff. *Fuck. No, this can't be happening.*

Make it stop. I would give anything to make it stop.

"But why?" I cry out, unable to keep the panic at bay. None

of this makes sense. "Why are you doing this?"

"You only had one question," he says dryly before the click of the door and a dull beep alert me that the driver's side door has opened.

Thump, thump, thump, my heart hammers.

A moment later, the door by my head opens. I can't help but scream as strong hands grip me under the armpits and Holden pulls me out of the car, forcing me stand up before taking my bound wrists in hand.

Fear consumes every inch of me, and it takes everything I have not to cry. Not to give him the fucking satisfaction.

"The ties I have won't hurt you," he says, "but I swear if you try and pull away, I'll have you on your knees choking yourself. I don't want to hurt you unless I have to ... Kiersten."

I freeze and turn my head toward Holden even though I'm still blindfolded. I can hear what sounds like industrial machinery in the distance, but other than that, we're alone as best I can tell.

A slight tug at my bonds convinces me that following him is the best option, and a moment later, he has me sit down on what feels like wood, cold wood in an even colder breeze. There's a *snap* sound, and I realize that my ties have been clipped to ... whatever this is. Faintly, I can hear water slapping against concrete, and outside the building, seagulls. "Now that we're alone and you're not going anywhere, let's talk."

Thump, thump, thump.

Holden removes my blindfold, and I squint as my eyes adjust. The lights are relatively dim, and other than a throbbing headache in the back of my skull, I'm able to look around.

I'm in a warehouse. Or at least, what looks like a warehouse, maybe some other type of small industrial building that has storage capabilities. Weak light filters in through grimy windows, and through an open space to my right is the ocean. "Where are we?"

"Where yelling or screaming won't help you," Holden assures me.

A chill runs down my spine. His voice is cold, with a restrained anger that sounds nothing at all like the young man I've known for years. "I promise you, Kiersten, you're not in trouble . . . yet. I just need you to answer a question for me, and then I'll go, disappear from your life, maybe."

"Maybe?"

Holden nods. "As long as you tell me which one of you killed my father."

I blink, stunned by the statement. Or maybe it's the headache, because I thought he just asked about . . . "What?"

"My father . . . Ivan Lewis," Holden repeats with his voice raised, and I feel my gut sink into my shoes, if I were still wearing shoes. "I thought it was Gabriel. He was the one who fled the country, after all. I thought he was the one who did it, and I've spent years tracking him down and trying to find him."

"You . . . you're Ivan's *son?*" Breath is stolen from me as the dominoes fall into place.

"You catch on so very fast," Holden says mockingly. "I thought you would know where Gabriel was. It was why I inserted myself into your operation. Then as time passed, I realized you didn't know shit, and it became sort of a waiting game. I never thought he'd come back to you. I didn't even know if he gave a shit about you anymore. I almost . . . almost lost hope. It's meant to be, don't you think?"

"What's meant to be, Holden?" I ask cautiously. My eyes meet his, and there is just anger in dark eyes that look back at me. "Are you going to kill him?"

"Most likely," Holden says almost agreeably, and my heart shatters. It takes everything in me not to show just how devastating his admission is. "Look, Kiersten. You know I have the skills to make you tell me what I want to know. Now personally, I like you. As Madam Lynn, you've always been good to me. So I'm taking that into consideration. Do *not* push me."

"So all those times you brought up your father . . ." I ask, every conversation we've ever had playing in my mind. "You couldn't have even been in kindergarten when he died."

"Actually, I was a baby," Holden admits. "I was only a baby. And my mother, she was left with nothing because of it. All the money was gone. We had nothing. All the money my father had made was tied up in ways that we couldn't get to. It took me a long time, but I uncovered what actually happened. You took a life from me that was supposed to be mine. You took everything from us."

"Holden," I reply, terrified as I jerk forward, but whatever he clipped my restraint to isn't letting go. Fear sinks its talons into me.

Holden ignores me and continues. "My mother lost her mind," he says, almost conversationally. "She was batshit by the time I was in grade school, and she finally killed herself when I moved out five years ago. My one regret in all I've done over the past twenty years, Kiersten, is that I never got the chance to tell her that I *found* you. That I found the source of all of this pain, and that I was going to find vengeance for my father's murder. Of all the things in the world . . . I fucking deserve that. Now, I'll say it again. Who killed him? Was it Gabriel . . . or was it you?"

Holden

Five years ago

The rain patters down on me as the small gathering breaks up. I guess I understand it, the lack of attendance. The last few years of her life, my mother wasn't exactly good company. One of the reasons I moved out, in fact, was that I had to make a choice.

Her life . . . or my life.

"You okay, son?" the priest asks me, patting me on the shoulder. "I know she was troubled, but she was still your mother."

"I'll be fine, Father," I assure him. "I know who caused this."

The priest sighs. He's heard me before, when I've talked with him in confession. It's the closest thing to therapy I can afford. "Holden, you know I cannot condone what you've talked with me about. Justice comes in God's time, not ours."

"No offense, Father, but if He is in any way *just*, he'll give me vengeance," I reply. Ignoring my mother's grave for a moment, I look at the marker next to it, a plain brass plaque on the turf. "Look at him, buried in a pauper's grave. We had so little when he died. We couldn't afford a fucking headstone. They took everything."

He parts his lips to speak, but I cut him off, rage getting the better of me.

"You know, for a few years there, I remember men would come by. Men who said they knew my father, that it was unfortunate what happened to him, but that things were going to be okay," I add, kneeling in the grass next to my father's grave marker.

"But those men, the stories they'd tell me . . . how they swore I'd have a place with them, running this city when I got older. That I'd be to them like my father was, but even better. They were liars, all of them. They just wanted to soothe their guilty consciences."

"Holden, holding onto this bitterness, this darkness . . . it will corrupt you." He emphasized, "Do not let the darkness corrupt you."

I chuckle softly. "Tell that to the judge who says I've got issues and I need to stay in a state-approved foster home until I turn eighteen."

"I can see what I can do about that if you'd like, Holden."

I shake my head, touching my father's grave marker before getting up. "Don't worry about it, Father. I'll be alright. They told me enough. I'll do what I must."

"Son—"

"Don't," I cut him off. I turn, lifting the collar on my coat up to cover my neck as I prepare to walk away. "I'm not going to let them get away with this."

Chapter 27

Gabriel

Present

My heart hammers and I can barely see straight. With white-knuckled fists, I resist the urge to punch the fucking window.

"Drive faster." I grit out the words as we speed down the highway, following the trace from Holden's phone before he either threw it or removed the card. Either way, we lost signal.

Her phone is back at the club. There's no way to trace them. All we know is he went down this highway before tossing his phone out. His intel shows he owns a single property this far up north. If they're not there . . . I'll never find them.

Hopelessness threatens and anger resonates as I yell, "Faster!" It's agony sitting in the goddamn passenger seat, my phone pinging with information upon information about Holden Jackson now known as Holden Lewis. He's Ivan's son. I never knew he even had a fucking son.

Joshua glances at me but pushes the accelerator a little harder.

There's nothing but agony to accompany us. We could be too late. My head falls back against the seat rest. It could all be too fucking late.

"Are you sure that you're making the right choice?" Joshua asks as the asphalt blurs. He gave me two choices.

"Joshua, if Holden wanted to talk, he could have talked. He could have approached me at any time one on one, if that was his intent. He took Kiersten." My voice cracks as fear riddles its way into every possible outcome.

Joshua nods and points toward the glove box. "Pistol." A beat passes as we turn off the highway. "Holden's well-trained."

There's not an ounce of hesitation in me. I see it all play out in my mind. The moment I see him, he's dead. There's no other option. My pulse races. Adrenaline screams in my veins. And I'm fucking stuck here, waiting to let it out.

Joshua follows the directions from his team, and all the while, I prepare to end this once and for all, remembering every moment I've ever had with her. Every little fight, every time she looked at me like she wanted to tell me she loved me but didn't. And the first time that we made love.

Emotions swell in my throat, and all I can do is to tell Joshua to drive faster.

If they aren't there, I think I may have lost her forever. The gun is heavy in my hand as the car slows down and the sun turns an auburn shade as it begins to set and allow darkness to take over.

We turn into a dockside warehouse district that is the sort of place where unfortunate things go down. I've owned a few buildings in places like this, and they're not pretty. They're dangerous, noisy, and exactly the sort of place where you can do bad things to people without anyone ever knowing about it.

"Stop here," I tell him, and Joshua shuts off the car and grabs his phone to bring up the warehouse layout. "He bought it the same time he started working for the club." Dread drifts into my blood as I stare at the old warehouse. There's a light on inside. There's hope.

I reach for the door handle but Joshua stops me. "A plan. One minute. Stay with me." All I can think is that every second we wait, she could die. I need to save her.

Chills run through me, and they only make me grip the gun tighter. Joshua speaks and I can barely hear him. He has a plan. One where I play a part. I get the message. My job is to get Holden's attention, get him talking. Then, while he's distracted, Joshua will come in from the side.

"The building's got two entrances," Joshua says, looking. "I'll go in the side door. You approach from the front. Holden could be expecting you, but he'll want to talk."

I nod, although I can barely focus. He stole her away from me. I have no idea what he's done to her. But there's no turning back. I swallow thickly as I open the car door.

Joshua points as the night gets darker, but I can still see him. The doors. My blood rages inside, the rushing in my ears all I can hear.

The main entrance of the warehouse is mostly closed, but I hear movement in the back. Doing the best I can to stay quiet, I slip under the door, trying to stay unnoticed yet move as quickly as I can.

I crawl through filth from the concrete floor, focusing on the dim light from a room ahead. My heart beats harder as the sounds filter in. Crying. She's crying.

Heat floods through me as I move faster. *She's alive. My Kiersten is alive.* The back hangar doors are raised, letting in the harsh, bitter air and the smell of open water.

Suddenly, I hear a choked gasp. "Hold—" It's then that the room comes into focus. A large space with nothing but freight boxes and them right in the center of a scene stolen from my nightmares. They're all the way toward the back, the furthest from me as they could possibly be. She struggles in his grasp.

On the other edge of the room, he has her, his arm around her neck and his grip tightening. "You were honest," he says as he lifts Kiersten off her feet.

Every muscle coils as I run ahead at full speed and without any care of being caught. "Holden!" I scream out, doing everything I can to make him look up. They're in the back and I'm too far away. "Holden!" My throat scorches as his name tears up it.

He doesn't. She struggles under him, and as she does, her eyes reach mine, bloodshot as she struggles to breathe.

My Kiersten. My love.

Every ounce of sense shatters. The world slows, and I know right then and there, she's going to die before I can get to her.

I don't think, I don't question myself. Instead, I come to a halt, lifting the pistol in my hand. My heart thumps. It's a clear shot as he leans back with her in a chokehold.

I aim for his head as her eyes roll back, and my hand trembles, but I squeeze.

One shot. *Bang.* I miss, and it's then that he sees me. Second shot.

He jolts back, her limp in his arms. The man staggers, a perfectly round hole in his jaw spilling blood down his throat. His eyes are vacant, and I fire another shot as he stumbles, still barely holding onto her. All the while, I keep moving, knowing full well that the door is wide open and the tide is right there.

As I race toward them, their bodies fall, both of them

silent. *Thump, thump.*

It's all in slow motion as he and Kiersten go tumbling into the water. Dropping my gun, I sprint over, screaming, "Kiersten!"

Reaching the edge of the water, I see her slip under, a bubble rising to mark where she fell. Ignoring everything else, I dive into the freezing cold water.

The freezing temperature is shocking, and I have no idea if she's even alive.

It's too dark to see. Too cold to feel. Terror strikes me to my core. *Thump, thump.*

His body is found first, his clothing floating in the water ahead of me. I shove past his lifeless corpse to find Kiersten in the murky depths. Seeing a flash of white, I grab and kick for the surface, bringing her with me.

Thump, thump.

I gasp for air and struggle to grip the edge of the dock and pull her up, soaking wet and barely cognizant.

Water drips down from the dock, and under the moonlight, I do everything I can to help her, all the while screaming for Joshua, screaming for help.

Surfacing, I can see the problem. He wrapped a rope around her neck as well. It looks like a bondage device, and something's still pulled tight. Reaching behind her neck, I grab the rope and pull up, giving her a little bit of slack.

"Gabriel." Joshua's voice slices through the fear as I

attempt to give Kiersten CPR. Hands on her chest, I breathe into her mouth. Her face is blue, her body still.

"Gabriel!" he screams, grabbing me, and in the dead of night, the sounds of tires and men yelling rings through. He has to rip me away and step in.

"She's not breathing," I barely get out. *Thump*, *thump*.

The fear of being too late is all that I can focus on as Joshua gives her CPR and then men hustle through the rundown warehouse.

We were too late. We were only a moment too late.

Chapter 28

Kiersten

"How is she, Doctor?"

"Bruised trachea, a bit of water in the lungs, but she'll live," the doctor says, putting his stethoscope away. He's a private doctor, Joshua assures us. With wrinkles around his eyes and gray at his temples, he's older and calmer. His calm disposition is welcoming in all the chaos.

"Where did you fall in the water again?"

"By the docks," I rasp, still shivering underneath the big, fluffy bathrobe Gabriel wrapped me in. The fire behind me blazes, and it's not the temperature of the room that chills me. It's warm and cozy in Gabriel's house. I just can't believe what happened, and every time I even think about it, I start shivering again.

Reaching into his bag, he pulls out two boxes. "Here. General antibiotic, and a wide spectrum antiparasitic agent, a seven-day regimen. Just in case." He hands them to Gabriel as I pull the robe tighter and try not to think about what happened. I almost died. If Gabriel hadn't pulled me out of the water and Joshua hadn't resuscitated me, I'd be dead just like Holden is.

"What'll it do to her?" Gabriel asks, pulling me back to the moment. He's still shaken up, in sweats and a white tee that clings to his shoulders, and clinging to me as if he'll never let me go. He wraps an arm around me, pulling my chest to his front as he talks to the doctor and I lean into his warmth.

It's over. He whispered to me the entire way back here. *It's over.*

It's really, truly over.

I can barely focus on the conversation at hand. All I can think is that it's done. And we survived.

"Take these for now," the doctor tells me, holding out his hand.

"Thank you, Doctor," I rasp, taking the meds. One's tiny and pink, looking almost like cake decoration candies, while the other's a plain white tablet. Setting them on the table, I wait as Joshua escorts the doctor out, locking the door behind him.

"I'll handle operations at the club tonight," Joshua says. "I'll also talk with Zander, explain to him the basics. Take a few days off. I'll have people securing this place."

"Joshua, no offense," Gabriel says, "but can they be trusted? You trusted Holden."

"And I'm going to be paying for that for a very long time," Joshua says simply, looking at me. "Kiersten, you're my business partner, yes. But you're also like a little sister to me. That I fucked up this badly . . . I'm sorry."

"We both fucked up," I reply, getting up and approaching Joshua. "I trusted him too. There's no guilt on your end. Let's talk tomorrow, please," I get out and then clear my throat. It hurts like hell.

Joshua nods, and a moment later, leaves. With the door closed behind him, it's just Gabriel and me in his house, and the silence is heavy between us. Since pulling me out of the water, I haven't said a word to him directly.

I don't know what to say or what to think, even. He comes back into my life, and within weeks, my life is already in chaos again. And this time, I almost died over it.

But he saved me. And all of this happened because of me.

"Kiersten, if you want me to leave . . . I will," Gabriel says quietly. "But if you'd let me stay, I want to stay."

There's so much concern in his voice, and while I'm still unsure of everything that happened, I know without a doubt that I love him. That I need him and that I'm grateful he's still here with me.

I can't help it. I love him. I've never stopped loving him.

"I need you to hold me and not let go. So don't you dare think about leaving me right now," I tell him in a cracked voice, and in return, he kisses me.

First, he's gentle, and my lips mold to his. Then more fiercely.

He only breaks the kiss to whisper in the warm air between us, "I'm so sorry, Kiersten."

His eyes are closed, and pain is clearly etched in his expression.

I can't take it. This torture needs to end for both of us.

With both of my hands on his jaw, I wait for him to look at me and I whisper back, "Don't be sorry, just love me."

"I love you so damn much."

"I love you too."

His hands come to my waist, and I wrap my arms around his neck, kissing him softly. He kisses me back, his chest hitching as he lets his emotions go, and I feel myself absorbed into him, not just his body but also his heart and soul.

It's meant to be delicate, but my touch turns needy, desperate to have him and know that I am truly his in every way. That nothing will come between us.

"I need you," I whisper into the warmth between us. Gabriel smiles, kissing my lips softly before making his way down my body.

His hands reach to the knot on my robe's belt, untying it and slipping the big, fluffy garment off my shoulders to puddle at my feet. Taking me in his arms again, we sink to the floor, cradled by the fluffy rug under our feet.

Spreading my legs, he looks me deeply in the eyes before lowering his lips and tasting me, kissing my pussy with his own desperate need. My eyes flutter, and I run my hand through his hair, my head falling back as the pleasure quickly builds. "Yes . . . right there. Right there."

He knows me, loving me tenderly with his lips and tongue as he kisses my center, stroking my folds and sucking my lips until I'm trembling on edge. Only then, when I'm at the edge of begging for more, does he stroke my clit with the tip of his tongue. I fall apart, whimpering softly as he makes me come with his feather-soft strokes.

I'm barely recovered when Gabriel kisses his way up my body, capturing my mouth again in a tender kiss as he positions himself at my entrance.

"I love you," he murmurs before he slips inside me.

We stare into each other's eyes as he fills me, rocking gently as he waits for me. I stroke the back of his neck, my lips parted in utter ecstasy from the sweet ache of him inside me, seeing the little flecks of gold that dot his irises and the warmth of his body pressing into me.

It feels like forever. "I need forever," I whisper, and I don't know why. Before I can second-guess, before I can take it back or feel insecure or vulnerable, he murmurs as he pushes in deeper, "You are my forever." I feverishly take his lips with mine and rock myself against him.

Slowly, he starts to stroke in and out of me, holding himself above me with his elbows until suddenly, he rolls us on the carpet, putting me on top of him.

Sitting up, I look down on my love and ride him slowly, feeling every ounce of pleasure. I rarely get on top with him, so every stroke of his cock and beat of our hearts sears itself into my memory.

The fire crackles again, and I ride faster, my ass slapping up and down lightly on Gabriel's hips as the tide rises again within me. I can feel him start thrusting up to meet me, our passion building together as he lets go of my thighs to entwine his fingers with mine.

My release finds me quickly, as his does for him. I throw my head back, my back arched and my hair cascading down my back as I fall into the abyss. I know what this means. There's no turning back. There's no path in my life that doesn't include Gabriel . . . but that's what I want.

I'm his.

He's mine.

And as I sag to his chest and we roll to lie side by side on the fluffy rug, I look into his eyes and I know one truth.

There's no other path I could ever want.

Epilogue

Gabriel

Two Months Later

Stepping through the doorway to the main dining room at Club X, I take a moment to adjust the mask over my eyes. It's still something I'm getting used to, and I'm still finding the exact mask to fit my taste.

The half-face mask is tight to my hairline and ears but stops at my nose. It's comfortable and to Kiersten's liking.

That's what I enjoy most about it. She blushes when she sees me in it, barely containing a seductive smile. It took a little time for her to recover, but my sweet submissive is flourishing and our new life is a dream I never dared to allow myself to have.

With my mask firmly in place, I brush the left lapel of my tuxedo, making sure everything's perfect before taking in the scene.

On stage, a Dom in black suit pants and a white T-shirt that shows off his muscular physique is currently tending to the very reddish ass of his sub.

Her moans are so loud that even from across the room I can tell she's in heaven. He rubs the lotion into her skin with gentle strokes, but I suspect that at least part of her bliss is from what looks like a vibrating U-shaped dildo currently in use.

An asymmetric grin pulls at my lips. It's the sort of aftercare that I definitely approve of.

A soft hiss comes from my left, and I watch a very skimpily clad submissive on her knees and between the legs of her Dom. He guides her with his left hand as she hollows her cheeks on his cock while sipping a drink with the other. They're clearly a couple that enjoys public displays. Other couples in the darkened room enjoy heavy petting. Some members are single and simply here to learn aftercare and paddle techniques. Madam Lynn certainly knows how to put on a show.

I watch the Dom and sub on stage finish their demonstration, all the while imagining Kiersten over my own lap. There's still so much for the two of us to try together. I have to step aside when the staff comes out with a fresh course of meals for the assembled group. How the kitchen staff handles a full five-course meal that members can start at any 'gap point' between entertainment acts is truly impressive.

Tonight's emcee, a man in a black suit but no mask to signify his employee status in the club, takes the mic. "Doms and subs, ladies and gentlemen, thank you. Your next course is coming. The next entertainment act will reconvene in twenty minutes."

The emcee leaves, and I make my way over to the other side of the room where I find Roland and two other men on duty. The added men to security are . . . excessive, but they blend in. They're officially 'probationary staff' for Club X under Joshua's command, and they're still learning the ropes.

"How are things?" I ask Roland, who's looking rather more put together than usual. His suit is form-fitted, probably custom-tailored. He's freshly shaven, and his hair is styled. It's . . . quite a different look for the man who's typically so casual. "Enjoying the new job?"

"I'm learning to deal with the distractions," Roland admits. "But tonight's my last night. I have another offer."

My first reaction is shock, and judging by his expression, my reaction is written on my face. I compose myself.

"It's a loss not to have you here," I reply, and Roland shakes his head. "No?"

"I said I'm leaving the job, not that I'm leaving Club X," Roland says quietly. "My new job pays well, and I've already talked to Joshua and Madam Lynn."

"You're joining Club X," I correct myself, and he nods.

"Someone tempted me into it," he comments, and his gaze shifts from me to the crowd.

"Who's the girl?" I ask, putting the pieces together.

"That obvious?" Roland asks, and I smirk. I know the look of a man who's got his heart somewhere beside his job. I see it in the mirror every morning. "Valerie. She's part of the next entertainment act, but she's unattached. The Dom and sub couple who are running the act asked her to join in because she's . . . flexible."

I chuckle and pat Roland on the shoulder. "Enjoy yourself."

"I will, thank you," Roland says. "By the way, will you be attending tomorrow night's auction? I was given an invitation by Madam Lynn."

"Will Valerie be going up for auction?" I ask, and Roland shakes his head. "No?"

"She told me that her collar can't be bought with cash," Roland says. "I'm interested in seeing if I have what it takes to earn it instead."

I smirk at her comment. I imagine Roland is going to have his hands full.

"Good. Best of luck," I reply and leave him to his business and me to mine.

Going up the spiral staircase behind Roland, I climb the steps to Madam Lynn's office, taking out my copy of the key that only she and I have. Slipping it into the lock, I turn the knob and step inside, locking the door behind me.

The room seems empty, and to a casual observer it might be. But after a moment, I hear the faint whir of a motor, something most people would think might belong to a desktop computer.

I know what the motor's for, though. "How is my little whore doing?"

Kiersten's response is moaned. "Sir." And I fucking love it.

I come around the desk, smiling at the image before me. Kiersten, her body trembling and flushed and my collar around her neck. She's folded in half, a slightly flexible padded PVC 'stick' keeping her ankles tucked behind her neck.

It turns her hips up and allows me to watch the vibrator I left inside her pump slowly, working its way in and out of her very needy pussy.

"It looks like you might be in need," I tease her, reaching forward and helping her remove her restraint. She collapses, her breasts heaving as I lay the stick aside, my cock rock hard and ready for her. "How can I make my submissive happy?"

"Mmm," Kiersten replies breathlessly, a grin on her lips. "Over the desk, please, Sir," she says. "My legs are a little tingly still."

I chuckle, lifting her up and aligning her just the way she asks before stripping off my tuxedo jacket and undoing my pants. My cock springs out at full attention, and with a single stroke I slide into her, remembering just how she likes it. Smooth as silk.

"Oh, God, Gabriel . . . fuck me please, Sir," she moans, and I pull back, stroking in again and again.

I quicken my pace, gripping her hips hard to keep her from bruising against the desk, my hips slapping against her ass. She gasps, and it fuels me to fuck her hard and rough.

She comes hard and fast, and as the pleasure rocks through her, she cries out my name. It's my undoing.

Kiersten shakes, and I pull her up, holding her through her release and whispering into the crook of her neck.

"I love you," I whisper again and again. "I love you."

When it passes, Kiersten turns in my arms, kissing me softly. "And I love you."

From the authors: an extra scene with *sharing* . . . to say thank you for reading. There's more to come!

Gabriel

The Past, June

On the TV screen, the two service academies pummel each other in a rivalry game. It means nothing to me, but I put it on because Davidson went to one of the universities.

Not that anyone's paying attention to the sixty-inch widescreen in my living room. And while there are vintage libations to be sampled from my wet bar and plenty of gourmet appetizers set out on sterling silver trays on the cherrywood table I had brought in for today's gathering, right now, every man in this room, six of them in total, is fixated on one sight.

One delectable, needy, hot and wanting sight.

Her eyes are covered with a strip of black silk, as they've been this entire gathering.

My business partners wanted to forego the masks, and so Kiersten proposed this alternative to me. With her hair styled in an upswept bun and her eyes covered, her expression is one of vulnerability but also desire.

One thing I've noticed is that she doesn't like to see them. She doesn't want to know who it is who's fucking her, and I always have to be in the room. She often searches me out and tempts me to kiss her, to tell her she's being a good girl. I fucking love it.

This arrangement, though . . . with her not seeing . . . it's new for her and it has me on edge.

Laid out on the kitchen counter, a small pillow beneath her head, her hands are free, although she opts to grip the edge of the marble, but her knees are pulled up, tied with matching silk in such a way that no matter what, she's available for every man to feast his eyes on her perfect body.

Her breasts are available for sucking and nipping, plucking and playing.

That was my idea, and a sign of trust in me that she's allowing it. Yes, she could release herself. The knots are just bows. But she doesn't. Instead, she listens to me when I tell her it's time for her to play, and she answers dutifully, the blush rising up her chest to her cheeks before reaching out on the counter for the vibrator, turning it on and placing it against her clit.

"Holy Jesus, Gabriel, she's so wet she's fucking glistening," Davidson says as in the background, a touchdown's kicked. He paces in front of her, a beer in one hand, and then he cocks his head. "Does she enjoy ass play?"

It's obvious that it turns her on when they talk about her in front of her.

It's obvious she enjoys being used and even a little degraded.

It's obvious she likes to be passed around like a fucking party favor.

Those are things I could never give her myself. It's a fantasy that requires other players. And one I never realized how much I'd enjoy until she asked me for it.

"How about you tell him, my little whore?" I reply, stroking Kiersten's hair. "Have you had your ass played with?"

"Yes Sir," she moans, pushing the vibrator down and bringing it down to tease her folds. She pushes it in, moaning as the thick silicone penetrates her and the vibrations pulse through her.

A tumbler falls to the thickly carpeted floor with the mutter of "shit." Some of the men laugh at him for being so damn distracted by a woman that he can't hold on to a glass. Another one of our guests groans, and I can't help but grin. "Look at how her tight cunt clenches even without anything in it," I mention, and the men gather, their composure lessening.

"So, about her ass?"

"Fuck her all you want. That's what she's here for." I make sure to add, "Within the rules. Isn't that right, my needy little whore?"

"Yes Sir," Kiersten moans as the vibrator pulses in her ass now. "I'm going to be a good little fuck toy for you and your friends."

She smiles shyly when the men chuckle. We've been together eight months at this point, and I know exactly how much this turns her on.

Attention half turns back to the game, but in between plays or during commercial breaks, one or more of my friends comes over, stroking her pussy lips or pushing the vibrator in and out of her ass.

She loves it, wiggling herself temptingly whenever she hears footsteps, and the sound of her coming as Richards decides that what he really needs isn't an appetizer but to lap at her pussy is exquisite.

"You like that, my little whore?" I ask her as Richards devours her, lapping in languid licks. "Is he good?"

"So good, Sir . . . fuck, Sir," she whimpers, and her tone rises before her back arches and she comes on his tongue. Richards moans himself, and I wonder if he's found his own release in his slacks. I wouldn't put it past him, and I don't mind.

He'll be ready again by the time halftime is over.

One by one, they come over, taking their turns to plunge

into her wet, clenching pussy or gaping ass. She takes it all, coming again and again and thanking them like I tell her to. It's fucking hot as hell.

Every so often, I ask her what her safe word is to remind her that she has it and to make sure she's cognizant.

Even when she's breathless, she answers. And every time she does, she tilts her head in longing. I kiss her each time and make sure I tell her what a good girl she is.

It's in those moments that she smiles a soft smile that she only shows me.

About the Authors

Thank you so much for reading our co-written novel. We hope you loved reading it as much as we loved writing it!

For more information on the books we have published, bonus scenes and more visit our websites.

More by Willow Winters
www.willowwinterswrites.com/books

More by Lauren Landish
www.laurenlandish.com

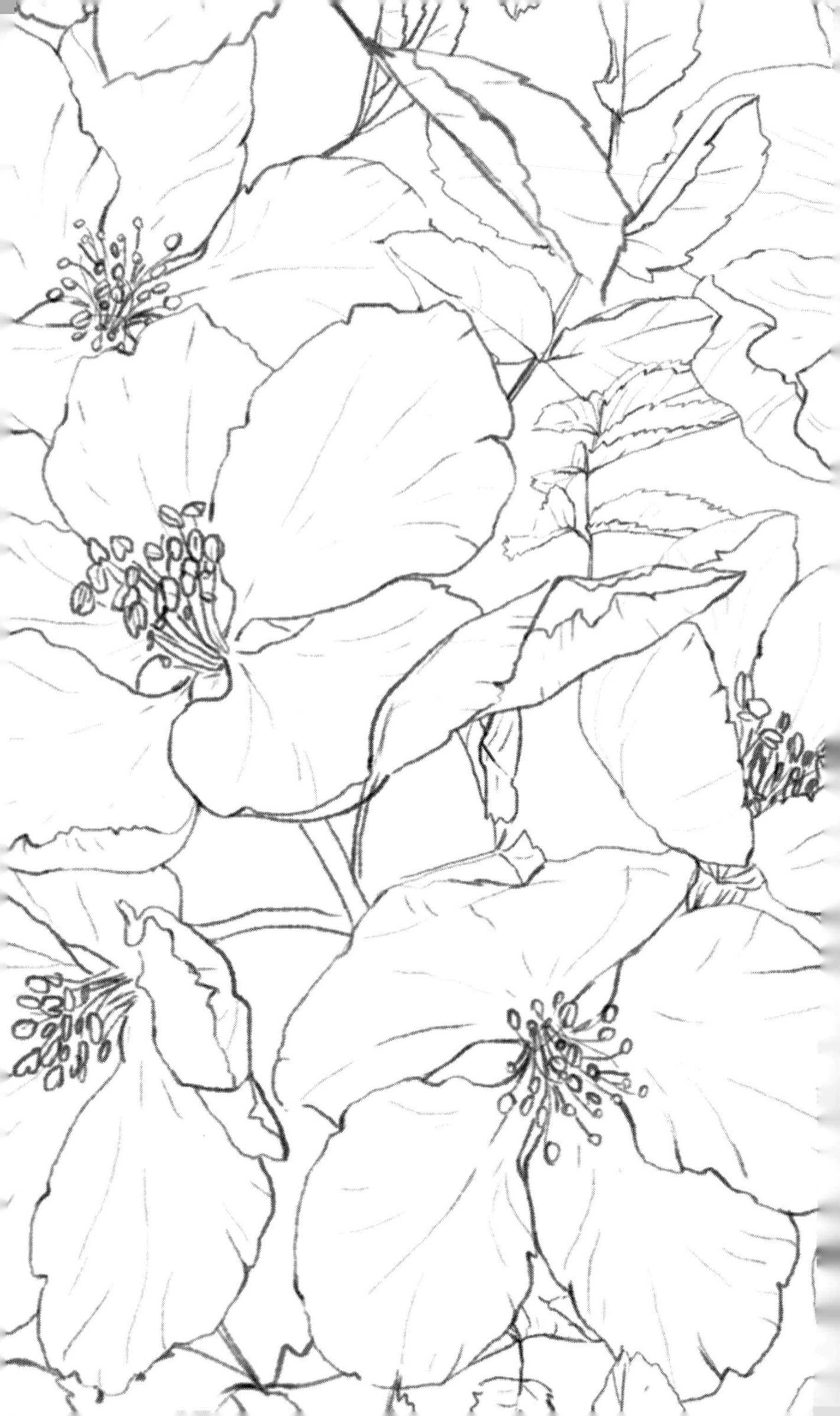

Printed in Great Britain
by Amazon